There was* something *in his tone, in the depths of his brilliant dark eyes.

Eyes say more than words ever can.

What were hers saying? That she wanted to leap up, go to him, hug him, tell him she had missed him *dreadfully* in spite of all the wonderful times she'd been having?

Common sense won over. This was Corin Rylance. Dalton Rylance's son and heir. A family worth billions. These were important people who mattered. Corin was way out of her league.

There can be no future in this, Miranda thought. *All you stand to gain is heartbreak.*

The lives and loves
of Australia's most powerful family

Growing up in the spotlight hasn't been easy,
but the two Rylance heirs,
Corin and his sister, Zara, have come of age
and are ready to claim their inheritance.

Though they are privileged, proud and powerful,
they are about to discover that there are some
things money can't buy….

This month meet Corin Rylance.
Super-handsome, super-rich, he's…

AUSTRALIA'S MOST ELIGIBLE BACHELOR

and he's got his eye on ordinary girl
Miranda Thornton!

Look out for Corin's sister Zara Rylance's
story, coming in October 2010!

CATTLE BARON NEEDS A BRIDE

MARGARET WAY

Australia's Most Eligible Bachelor

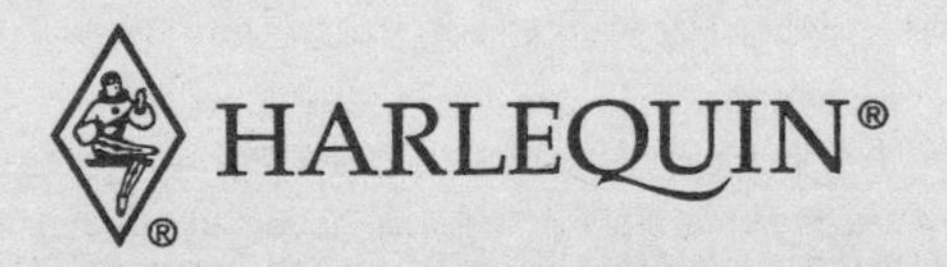

TORONTO • NEW YORK • LONDON
AMSTERDAM • PARIS • SYDNEY • HAMBURG
STOCKHOLM • ATHENS • TOKYO • MILAN • MADRID
PRAGUE • WARSAW • BUDAPEST • AUCKLAND

Recycling programs
for this product may
not exist in your area.

ISBN-13: 978-0-373-17679-3

AUSTRALIA'S MOST ELIGIBLE BACHELOR

First North American Publication 2010.

This edition published by arrangement with Harlequin Books S.A.

For questions and comments about the quality of this book please contact us at Customer_eCare@Harlequin.ca.

www.eHarlequin.com

Printed in U.S.A.

Margaret Way, a definite Leo, was born and raised in the subtropical river city of Brisbane, capital of the Sunshine State of Queensland. A conservatorium-trained pianist, teacher, accompanist and vocal coach, she found that her musical career came to an unexpected end when she took up writing—initially as a fun thing to do. She currently lives in a harborside apartment at beautiful Raby Bay, a thirty-minute drive from the state capital, where she loves dining alfresco on her plant-filled balcony, overlooking a translucent-green marina filled with all manner of pleasure craft—from motor cruisers costing millions of dollars and big, graceful yachts with carved masts standing tall against the cloudless blue sky to little bay runabouts. No one and nothing is in a mad rush, and she finds the laid-back village atmosphere very conducive to her writing. With well over one hundred books to her credit, she still believes her best is yet to come.

PROLOGUE

Brisbane, State Capital, Queensland.
Three years earlier.

FOR Miranda in her hyped-up state, everything seemed to be *rushing* at her: cars, buses, cabs, pedestrians. Even her blood was whooshing through her veins. The city seemed incredibly noisy—the pulse and beat of traffic, the mélange of sight and sound. Just to top it off, there was the threat of a late-afternoon thunderstorm, routine for high summer. Heat was vibrating rapidly to and fro between the forest of tall buildings, bouncing down on to the pavements. This was the norm: expectation of a brief, hectic downpour, then the return of a sun that admitted no rival. The overhead sky was still a dazzling deep blue, but there were ominous cracklings in the distance, the odd detonation of thunder and a bank-up of dark, silver-shot clouds with acid-green at their heart on the invisible horizon.

She was abuzz with adrenalin. Almost dancing with nerves. The humidity in the atmosphere did nothing to bank her intensity. The crowded street was thick with voices. People were milling about, smiling and chattering, happy to be going home after a long day at work; others were laden with shopping bags, feeling slightly guilty about blowing the budget on things they didn't need; more held mobile phones glued to their ears, their side of the conversation loud enough to make the deaf sit up and take notice! Hadn't they woken up to the fact mobile phones were a potential health hazard?

Of course there were dangers everywhere—even crossing the busy intersection. She could see the born-to-take-a-risk oddballs and the habitual stragglers caught halfway across the street at the red light. Ah, well! She couldn't talk. Consider the dangerously risky move she was determined on making this very afternoon, given a stroke of luck? She only had one chance to get it right, but she had thought it through very carefully.

Over the last fortnight it had become routine surveillance, checking on the comings and goings of the Rylance men. Billionaire father Dalton Rylance, Chairman and CEO of Rylance Metals, one of the biggest metal companies in the world, and his only son and heir, Corin. Corin Rylance, twenty-five, was by all accounts the perfect candidate to inherit the Rylance empire. The Crown Prince, as it were. Super-rich. Super-handsome. Super-eligible. An opinion echoed countless times by the tabloids and gushing women's magazines. That didn't mean, however, the Rylances were nice people.

Anger merged with her constant grief. *Not* nice was starkly true of the present Mrs Rylance—Leila—Dalton Rylance's glamorous second wife. His first wife had died in a car accident when Corin Rylance was in his early teens and his sister Zara a couple of years younger. A privileged life cut short. A few years later Dalton Rylance had shocked everyone by marrying a young woman from the PR section at Head Office called Leila Richardson. A gold-digger and an opportunist, according to family and friends who didn't know anything about this young woman, however good she was supposed to be at her job. Collective wisdom had it she hailed from New Zealand.

Yet the marriage had survived. With all that money behind it, why not? Always beautiful, Leila Rylance, polished to within an inch of her life, had become over a few short years a bona fide member of the Establishment. She might have been born into one of the best families herself. Except Leila Rylance must live her glamorous life always looking over her shoulder. Leila Rylance wasn't who she claimed she was.

Leila Rylance was a heartless monster.

It took some nerve to tackle people like the Rylances, Miranda thought for the umpteenth time. She could get into very serious trouble. These were people who took threats and perceived threats very seriously. They had armies of people working for them: staff, bodyguards, lawyers, probably they even had the Police Commissioner on side. She had to think seriously of being arrested, restraining orders and the like—the shame and humiliation—only she was fired up by her massive sense of injustice. Seventeen she might be, but she was clever—hadn't that tag been hung on her since she was knee-high to a grasshopper?

"Miranda is such a clever little girl, Mrs Thornton. She must be given every chance!"

That from a stream of teachers—the latest, her highly regarded headmistress, Professor Elizabeth Morgan, reeling off her achievements. Professor Morgan had great hopes Miranda Thornton would bring credit on herself and her school. She had done her bit. She had secured the highest possible score for her leaving certificate, excelling at all the necessary subjects she needed for her goal: Mathematics, Physics, Chemistry, Biology. She had admittance to the university of her choice. She had the *brain* and the strong desire to become a doctor, but it would be hard, if not downright impossible, to get through the science diploma necessary for med school without *money*. She had long set her sights on Medicine.

"Where do you suppose that's come from then, Tom? Our little Miri wanting to be a doctor?"

Her mother had often asked her father that question, wonderment in her tone. There was no medical background on either side of the family. Just ordinary working-class people. No one had made it to university.

But she had things going for her. She was resourceful. She had a maturity beyond her years. She coped well under pressure. That came directly from having looked after her mother for the last three years of her life battling cancer. The agony of it! To make it much worse, her death had come only a year or so since her hard-working father had died of a sudden massive heart attack. They had not been a young couple. Miranda was, in fact, a mid-life baby. Her mother had been forty-two when she fell pregnant, at a time when both her parents had despaired of ever producing a living child after a series of heartbreaking miscarriages.

Her childhood had been a happy, stable. They'd lived in a glorious natural environment. There had never been much money, and few of life's little luxuries, but money was by no means essential for contentment. She'd loved and been loved, the apple of her parents' eyes. Her parents had owned and run a small dairy farm in sub-tropical Queensland—the incredibly lush Hinterland behind the eastern seaboard, with the magnificent blue Pacific Ocean rolling in to its shores and only a short drive away. The farm had rarely shown more than a small profit. But they'd got by, working very hard—she included—to secure the best possible education at her prestigious private school for her final four years.

She would never forget the sacrifices her parents had made. In turn she had been fully committed to looking after them as they aged. Only now they were gone. And her world was lying in great jagged piles of rubble around her feet.

Her parents hadn't been her parents at all.

They'd been her *grandparents*.

And no one had told her.

She had grown up living a lie.

Her heartbeat was as loud as a ticking clock, pumping so fast it was almost choking her. The sun flashing off windscreens temporarily blinded her. She blinked hard. Turned her head.

Then she *saw* him.

Eureka! She was close. Soooo close!

One had to fight fire with fire. She braced herself, lithe and as swift on her feet as a fleet fourteen-year-old boy. He was coming out of the steel-and-glass palace of Rylance Tower. The son. What a stroke of luck! She would know him anywhere. His image was etched into her brain. Who could miss him anyway? He was tall, dark, stunningly handsome with a dazzling white smile. The ultimate chick-magnet, as her friend Wynona would say. Could have been a movie star only for his layer of gravitas. Unusual at his age. But then he was a mining magnate's son and heir, with a brilliant career ahead of him.

Well, he wasn't the only one going places, she thought. Her whole body was shaking with nervous energy. She hadn't been exactly sure she could deal with the father anyway. He was a hugely important man and purportedly ruthless. The odd thing was she had no real desire to potentially cause a break-up in his marriage. The son would do, whiz kid that he was, by far the less problematic proposition. Sometimes you just got *lucky*!

She watched the silver Rolls slide into the loading zone

outside the building as per usual. The grey-uniformed chauffer stepped out smartly—God, a uniform, in *this* heat?—going around the bonnet of the gleaming car to be at the ready to open the rear door for the supremo's son.

Couldn't he open it himself, for goodness' sake? Well, it did give the chauffeur a job. Every nerve in her body was throbbing with a mix of anticipation and a natural fear of the consequences. She had to get to him, speak to him, if her life was to go forward as she and her grandparents had planned. She watched Rylance dip his splendid crow-black head to get into the back seat of the car. This was the crucial moment. She seized it, taut as an athlete at the starter's gun. Before the chauffeur could make a move to close the door, she literally sprang into the vehicle in one excited leap, the wind lifting her skirt and showing the full length of her legs, landing in a breathless heap against the shoulder of her target, who was playing it very cool indeed.

"Hi there, Corin!" she cried breathlessly. "Remember me? The Beauman party? Didn't mean to scare you, but we have to talk."

Those kinds of words usually made young men sit up and pay attention.

The chauffeur, well-built, probably ex-army, leaned into the Rolls, concern written all over him. "You know this young lady, Mr Rylance?"

She smiled up at the grim-faced man, who appeared on trigger alert. "Of course he does. Don't you, Corin?"

Recognition didn't light up his brilliant dark eyes. "Convince me."

His speech was very clipped—blistering, really. Before she knew what he was about his lean, long-fingered hand snaked out, ran deftly but with delicacy over her shoulder, then down over her bodice, sparking her small breasts to life. She was shocked to the core, her entire body flooded with electricity. Even her nipples sprang erect. She prayed he didn't register that. He continued to frisk her to her narrow waist, cinched as it was by a wide leather belt. Mercifully he stopped there. Not a full body search, then. She was wearing a short summer dress, well above her knees. Sleeveless, low-necked. Nowhere to hide anything. Nowhere decent anyhow.

He grabbed her tote bag and handed it over to the grim-faced chauffeur. "Check the contents, Gil."

"You're joking!" she railed. "Check the contents? What are you expecting, Corin? A Taser? I'm absolutely harmless."

"I don't think so." Rylance kept a firm hold on her while the chauffeur swiftly and efficiently searched her bag.

"Nothing here, sir," he reported with a note of relief. "Usual girly things. And a few old snapshots. Shall I send her on her way, or call the police?"

"And tell them what, Gil?" Her voice, which had acquired a prestige accent from school, was laced with sarcasm. "Your boss has been waylaid by a five-three, hundred-pound seventeen-year-old he doesn't seem to remember? Why, a twelve-year-old boy could wrestle me to the ground. Trust me, Corin." She turned a burning scornful glance on Rylance. "You don't want anyone else in on our little chat, do you? Tell your man to pull over when we're clear of the city. Then Gil here can go for a nice stroll. A park would be fine. There's one on Vine."

Women were always chasing him. Hell, it went with the territory. But never had one taken a spectacular leap into his car. That was a first. He couldn't believe it. Not even after years of being hotly pursued. It was the money, of course. Every girl wanted to marry a billionaire, or at the very least a billionaire's son. But this was a *kid*! She'd said seventeen. She could be sixteen. Not *sweet*. She looked a turbulent little thing, even a touch dangerous, with her great turquoise-green eyes and a fiery expression on her heart-shaped face. A riot of short silver gilt curls clung to her finely sculpted skull. She had very coltish light limbs, like a dancer; she was imaginatively if inexpensively dressed. Had he met her anywhere at all, he would definitely remember. No way was she *unmemorable*. And she had beautiful legs. He couldn't help but notice.

So who the hell was she and what did she want? He had a fleeting moment when she put him in mind of someone. Who? No one he knew had those remarkable eyes or the rare silver-gilt hair. He was certain the colour was real. No betraying dark roots. Then there was her luminous alabaster skin. A natural blonde. Then it came to him. She was the very image of one of those mischievous sprites, nymphs, fairies—whatever. His sister, Zara, had used to fill her sketchbooks with them when she was a child. Zara would be intrigued by this one. All she needed was pointed ears, a garland of flowers and forest leaves around her head, and a wisp of some diaphanous garment to cover her willowy body.

They rode in a tense silence while he kept a tight hold on her arm. No conversation in front of the chauffeur. Some ten minutes out of the CBD the chauffeur pulled up beside a small park aglow with poincianas so heavy in blossom the great branches dipped like the tines of umbrellas. "This okay, sir?" The chauffeur turned his head.

"Fine, thanks, Gil. I'll listen to this enterprising young

woman's story—God only knows what that might be—then I'll give you a signal. I have a dinner party lined up for tonight."

"Of course you have!" said Miranda, still trying to recover from the shock of his touch and his nearness. She understood *exactly* now what made him what he was. He even gave off the scent of crisp, newly minted money.

The chauffeur stepped out of the Rolls, shut the door, then made off across the thick, springy grass to a bench beneath one of the trees. If Gil Roberts was wondering what the hell this was all about he knew better than to show it. He believed Corin implicitly when he said he didn't know the girl. He had been with the family for over twelve years, since Corin Rylance had been a boy. He had enormous liking and respect for him. Unlike a couple of his cousins, Corin was no playboy. He did *not* fool around with young girls, however enchanting and sexy. Maybe it had something to do with one of his cousins? A bit of blackmail, even? She had better not try it. Not on the Rylances.

"So?" Corin turned on her, his tone hard and edgy. "First of all, what's your name? You obviously know mine."

"Who doesn't?" she retorted, not insolently, but with some irony. "It's Miri Thornton. That's Miranda Thornton."

"Amazing—Miranda! Of course it would be." He didn't mask the sarcasm.

"What's that supposed to mean?" She stared at him with involuntary fascination. She was experiencing the weirdest feeling there was no one else in the world but the two of them. Imagine! Was she a total fool? She almost forgot what she was about with those dark eyes on her. God, he was handsome. The glossies were right. Up close and personal, his aura was so compelling it had her near gasping. It wasn't simply the good looks, it was the force field that surrounded him. It had picked her up with a vengeance. For the first time she felt intimidation.

"You're a smart girl," he was saying.

"Not a little twit?"

He ignored that. "Well educated, obviously. Miranda—Prospero's daughter?"

Deliberately she opened her eyes wide. "Got it in one. *The Tempest.* You know your Shakespeare. From whence did Corin come?" she asked with mock sweetness. "*Coriolanus?* Noble Caius Marcus?"

"Cut it out." His tone was terse. There was a decided glitter in his eyes, so dark a brown they were almost black. "I don't have time for this. What's it all about? You have exactly five minutes."

"Give me *one*," she retorted smartly, hoping she looked a whole lot more in control of herself than she was. "May I have my bag?"

He frowned at her. "What is it you want to show me?" He didn't oblige, but drew the tote bag onto his lap. Gil would have checked carefully, but there were always surprises in life. This extraordinary young woman didn't exactly look unstable or wired. He could see the high intelligence in her face, the keenness of her turquoise-green regard. She was *nothing* like all the well-connected young women he knew. The pressure was on him from his father to pick out a suitable bride. Annette Atwood was highly suitable. But did he honestly believe in *love*?

"Photographs." Miranda's mind was momentarily distracted while she focused on his hands. He had beautifully shaped hands. Hands were important to her.

"That's nice!" He didn't hide the mockery.

"I'd hold the *nice* until you have a look at them," she warned. "Don't think for one minute it's porn. Good old Gil would have spotted that, and I don't deal in such things. I was very well brought up. Go on—pull them out. They won't bite you."

"The cheek of you!" he gritted. "You know what I'd really like to do with you?" He was uncomfortably aware his body was coiled taut. Why? She was pint-sized. No physical threat at all. What *did* he want to do with her? Why was he giving her the time of day? Actually, he didn't *want* to think it through. She was so *young*, with her life in front of her. Despite himself he felt a disturbing level of attraction.

"Throw me out onto the street?" she was suggesting. "You could do it easily."

"Maybe I will at some point." He withdrew several photographs from a side pocket in her well-worn bag. They looked old, faded, turning up at the edges. He narrowed his dark eyes. "What exactly are these? Photographs of Mummy when she was a girl?" He was being facetious. Until he saw what he had in his hand.

God, no! This wasn't real. It couldn't be. It wasn't *her.* The girl in the photographs didn't just bear a strong resemblance to his stepmother. She *was* Leila—unless she had an identical twin.

"How clever of you, Corin," Miranda said, making an effort to conceal her own upset. "They're photographs of my mother when she was a year younger than I am now."

His expression turned daunting for so young a man. Shades of the father, Miranda supposed. "Just be quiet for a moment," he ordered.

Miranda knew when it was time to obey. She and Corin Rylance had polarised positions in life. She was a nobody. He was on the highest rung of society. Heir to a great fortune. He could cause her a lot of grief.

"So what's your game?" He shot her a steely glance, the expression in his fine eyes in no way benevolent.

"No game." She turned up her palms. "I'm deadly serious. We can keep this between the two of us, if you like. I'm certain from what I know of my birth mother—*your* stepmother—that she hasn't confided her sordid little story to another living soul. Least of all your father."

"You want money?" The stunning features drew tight with contempt.

"I *need* money," she corrected.

"Aaah! A big difference." The tone was withering.

"I think you can spare it."

"Do you, now?" His tone all but bit into her soft flesh. "So I'm to look after you indefinitely? Is that the plan? Well, let me help you out here, Miranda, as you're barely out of school. Blackmail is a very serious crime. I could turn you over to the police this afternoon. It would only take one call."

"Sure. I've risked that," she admitted. "But you won't be doing your family any favours, Corin. Don't think I'm not ashamed to have to ask you. I *have* to. My mother—*your* stepmother, your father's *wife*—owes me. I can't go to her. I loathe and despise her. She abandoned me when I was only a few weeks old."

"You can prove it?" His voice was harsh with unsuppressed emotion. "Or is this some highly imaginative ploy to make money?" The flaw in that was he could well see Leila doing such a thing. The only person Leila cared about was herself. Not his father. Although his father, business giant that he was, was in sexual thrall to her.

"I'm not stupid," Miranda said. "I'm not a liar or a con artist. Of course I can." She had to swallow hard on a sudden rush of tears. "I was brought up by my grandparents—my mother's parents—believing I was theirs. A change of life baby. Both of them are now dead. My grandmother very recently. She told me the truth on her deathbed. She wanted to make a clean breast of it. The last years of her life were terrible. She died of cancer."

His expression softened at the very real grief he saw in the depths of her crystalline eyes. "Miranda, I'm sorry, but your mother must have had a reason for doing what she did. That's if these photographs *are* of my stepmother. People do have doubles in life." Even as he said it he *knew* it was Leila.

"You know in your bones they are," Miranda told him bleakly. "I even look a teeny bit like her, don't you think?"

"Not really, no. Maybe the point to the chin—although Leila's is less pronounced."

"So I must have my father's colouring." There was a yearning note in her voice he picked up on. "Whoever he might be. She never would say. Anyway, I have a whole scrap-book if you want to see it. My birth mother was adored. My grandparents were lovely people. Yet she cut them—her own mother and father—ruthlessly out of her life. *I* didn't matter at all. Good gracious, no. I was just a huge mistake. You know how it is. She wasn't going to allow an unwanted baby to ruin her life. She ran away and never came back. Not even a postcard to say she was okay."

"You're sure about that?" he asked grimly. "Your grand-mother mightn't have told you everything. People have secrets. Some they take to the grave."

"Tell me about it," Miranda countered with real sadness. "I loved Mum—Sally—my grandmother. I nursed her. I was with her at the end. She told me everything. Not a pretty story. I had to forgive her. I loved her. She was so good to me. Yet the person I had trusted more than anyone else in the world had lied to me. God, it hurt. It will always hurt."

"I imagine it would." He studied her downbent face. She

had a lovely mouth, very finely cut. Leila's mouth was positively *lush*. This girl wore no lipstick. Maybe a touch of gloss. "I expect your grandmother thought it was best at the time. Then it all got away from her. Where did you live?"

She told him. "The Gold Coast Hinterland, Queensland."

"A beautiful area. I know it well. So your grandparents were farming people?" he asked with a frown. "According to Leila she was born in New Zealand."

"She was. And just look at how far she has come." Miranda gave a theatrical wave of her hands. "Married to one of the richest men in the country. You can bet your life she didn't want any more children. She's only thirty-three, you know. But children would only cramp her style."

True of Leila. "The woman you claim is your mother told my father she wasn't able to have children," he volunteered.

"I think you can take it she's a born liar. Anyway, your father has you and your sister. *You're* the heir."

"You bet your life I am."

"Don't look at *me*!" She slumped back against the rich leather upholstery. "*I* don't want to muscle in."

"I thought you did."

He had very sexy brackets at the sides of his mouth. "No way!" She shrugged, unsettled by his proximity. In a matter of moments this stranger had got under her skin. Definitely not allowed. "What I want—what I *need*—is to have the financial backing to get through med school. I'm clever. Maybe I'm even cleverer than you." She held up her hand. "Okay, joke! But I scored in the top one per cent for my finals."

"And there I was, only winning a few spelling bees."

"Not so." She sat straight. "You were awarded a university medal. You have an Honours Degree in Engineering. You also have a degree in Business Administration."

"Go on—what else?" he asked caustically.

"Listen, Corin. I did my homework. It was necessary. I'm not asking for a fortune, you know. I'll get a part-time job. Two if I have to. But I must attain my goal. It's what my par—my *grandparents* lived and worked for. I was the one who was to be given every chance. Only they both went and died on me. That's agony, you know."

He regarded her for a moment in silence, all kinds of emotions nipping at him fiercely. This girl was getting to him. And she had done it so easily. "Your story has to be checked out very thoroughly," he said. "You might tell me *how*, given there wasn't much money in the family, your mother got away? Everyone needs money to survive. She was just a schoolgirl. How did she manage?"

"I daresay she blackmailed my father," she said, bluntly rephrasing the explanation her grandmother had offered.

"So it runs in the family, then?"

She winced, her turquoise-green eyes flashing. "Don't make me hate you, Corin."

He laughed, very dryly. "That's okay. Hate works for me, Miranda."

Some note in his voice sent a shiver down her spine. "Miri, please."

He continued to scan her face. "I prefer Miranda."

She was locked into that brilliant regard. "You'll find I'm telling the truth right down to the last detail. My grandparents didn't know who fathered Leila's child. But, whoever it was, his family must have had money. Someone must have given it to her. Although she took *everything* she could lay her hands on from her parents, including much needed money that was awaiting banking."

"It's a terrible story, Miranda, but not rare," he said. "Young people—girls and boys—go missing all the time, for any number of reasons. It must be heartbreaking for the caring parents."

"Leila obviously didn't care about *them*. There was no abuse, no excessive strictness, only love. You know, I've been thinking of you—your father and you, certainly Leila—as the enemy," she confessed. "*You're* not so bad."

"You don't know me," he said.

"I know you bear a noble name. The Corin bit anyway. I like it. I don't even mind being allied with you, or *your* part of the enemy. But you can't be slow about this, Corin. There are lots of things to be taken care of. I don't have another damned soul in the world to appeal to."

"And I'm supposed to care?" He was out to test her.

"But you *do* care, don't you?" She was looking into his eyes as if she was reading his mind. "Leila may have cast a spell on your father, but I bet she didn't cast any spell on you or your sister."

Nothing could be truer. They had disliked and distrusted Leila even before she had married their father. Now they hated her. "So you think this will give me an advantage?" Of course it would. But he knew he wouldn't use it. Not *yet*, anyway. His moment would come.

"Nothing so ugly," she said. "You may dislike Leila. But you love your father. That's it, isn't it?"

"You might well make a doctor, Miranda," he answered tersely. "You appear to have a gift."

She visibly relaxed. "I hope so. I want so much to do good in this world. I won't let my paren—" she corrected herself again "—grandparents down. I'm going to see this through and you've got to help me. I've even had a psychological assessment to determine whether I have the right stuff to become a doctor."

"And you passed?"

"With flying colours, Corin. Also the mandatory interview for selection into the MBBS course. You don't mind if I call you Corin?"

"Obviously you have a keen interest in getting me to like you."

"I like you already. Bit odd, really. But I believe in destiny, don't you? I was waiting for you—maybe your father. I got you. Far and away the better choice."

There was severity, but a touch of amusement in his expression. "You can say that again. My father would have had you thrown out of the car. Right on your pretty ear."

"Is that so? You can tell a lot about a man by the way he treats a woman."

"I agree."

"Hey, you do love your dad, don't you?" She eyed him anxiously. There was something a bit *off* in his tone.

"Why do you ask that?"

"Unusual answer, Corin." She spoke in an unconscious clinical fashion. "I'd say textbook father-son conflict?"

"Sure you don't want to go for psychiatry?" he asked very dryly.

"I hit a nerve. Sorry. I'll back off. Anyway, even your father wouldn't have thrown me out. Not when I waved the photographs." His handsome face was near enough to hers to touch. "I have to be tough. Like you people. I know you can work this out somehow. I won't interfere. All you have to do is make it so I'm able to get through my first three years of training until I attain my BS, then I'll tackle my MB."

"An extremely arduous programme, Miranda," he warned her, shaking his head. Two of his old schoolfriends had dropped out in their second year, finding the going too tough. "Sure you're up to it? I'll accept you have the brains. Maybe you can handle the ton of studying required. But there's a lot of evidence many students leaving high school with top scores fall by the wayside for any number of reasons. Happens all the time."

She nodded in agreement, but with a degree of frustration. She had been warned many times over how tough it was. "Listen, Corin, you don't have to tell me. I know how hard it's going to be. I know many drop out. But it's not going happen to me. I mightn't look it, but I'm a stoic. I've had to be. My grandparents' hopes and dreams will prevail. I'm up for it."

Everything seemed to point to it. "Where do you intend to study?" he asked.

"Griffith for my BS, then on to UQ. Why do you look like that? I promise you I won't ever bother you. You need never lay eyes on me again."

"Sorry!" He focused his brilliant dark gaze on her. "*If* you check out—and it's by no means a foregone conclusion—you'll be expected to take tests I'll arrange. Again, *if* you pass our criteria you'll be under constant scrutiny. You mustn't think you've got this all sewn up, Miranda."

"If you want references you can contact my old school principal," she suggested eagerly, her heart beating like a drum.

"You just leave that to me." He dismissed her suggestion. "You'd be very foolish to try to put anything across me."

"Whoa…I gotcha, Corin." She held up her palms, her heart now drumming away triple-time. "So, you want to think it over?" She swallowed down her nerves, moistening her dry lips with the tip of her tongue.

"Of course I want to think it over." He spoke more sharply than he'd intended, but this girl was seriously sexy. God knew what power she'd have in a few years' time. "I may *sense* you're telling the truth. That's all. *If* you're Leila's daughter, as you claim, you could be an accomplished liar."

That made her heart swell with outrage. "What an absolutely rotten thing to say, Corin."

"Okay, I apologise." The glitter of tears stood in her beautiful eyes. Against all his principles, against rhyme and reason, even plain common sense, he had a powerful urge to catch that pointed chin and kiss her. Long and hard. A mind-body connection. It was almost as though he was being directed by another intelligence. Mercifully he had enough experience, let alone inbred caution, not to give way to an urge that was fraught with danger. Women had been making fools of men since time immemorial. Maybe this slip of a girl was trying to make a fool of *him*?

At first when she had made her mad leap into the car his mind had immediately sprung to his cousin, Greg. Greg was forever getting himself into trouble with women, but not teenagers—at least not to date. He'd never thought in a million years this would have something to do with Leila.

"Do you drive?" He turned his attention back to the would-be doctor. That counted for a lot with him. He had the ability to read people. She was ambitious, which he liked, idealistic, and she appeared very sincere in her aim. Becoming a doctor was a fine goal in life. He should check out her driver's licence. If she had one.

"I *can* drive," she confided. "As good as your Gil. Bet he was in the army at some stage. I used to drive the ute around the farm all the time, but I don't have a car. I can't afford one. Listen, Corin, I'm dirt-*poor* at the moment."

"So where do you live now?" he asked. Gil *was* ex-army. She was very sharp.

"I share a flat with friends. A major downgrade for us all,

but we have fun. My grandfather's dying was a nightmare, then my…grandmother. What money there was simply went in to the bottomless hole of medical costs. There's no licence for you to check. But you can check me out at my old school. I was Head Girl, no less Professor Morgan thought the world of me, which is as good a character reference as you're likely to get. You can check out my grandparents too. Needless to say everyone in the district believed me to be their mid-life child. I have more information on my birth mother if you want it. My grandmother knew all about her marrying your father. She read about it in the newspapers. Leila might be all dolled up, but she's the same Leila. Mum used to keep cuttings. Isn't that sad? A parent is always a parent. No matter what."

His father hadn't been much of one, he thought bleakly. Not much of a husband either. In fact, the powerful and ruthless Dalton Rylance was a major league bastard. But he was still madly infatuated with the very much younger Leila. Obsessed with her, really.

"It's all sad, Miranda."

He gave way to a dark sigh. He and Zara had been devastated when their mother had been killed. Their father's infidelities and lack of attention had brought great unhappiness to their beautiful, gentle mother. His maternal grandparents, the De Laceys, major shareholders in Ryland Metals, had positively loathed their son-in-law as much as they loved their daughter's children. He, as his mother's only son, had been extremely protective of her—ready to tell his father off at the drop of a hat, no matter the consequences. And there were quite a few he'd had to suffer along the way. The reality was he and Zara had looked to their mother for everything. Love, support, long serious discussions about life—where they were going. It was she who had taken them on numerous cultural outings. She'd been the source of joy in their so called privileged life. Their father had never been around. Jetting off here, off there. Legitimate business concerns, it had to be said, but it had never occurred to him to try to make up for his many absences when he returned. In his way Dalton Rylance had betrayed them all: his wife, his son and heir, and his daughter—the image of their beautiful mother.

And he punished her for it. Zara, the constant reminder. His hands tightened until his knuckles showed white.

"So what are *you* in the grip of?"

Her voice, which amazingly showed concern, brought him out of his dark thoughts.

"What do you mean?" She was way too perceptive, this girl.

"Don't bite my head off, Corin. It can't be *me*. It's someone else you're thinking about. What did you and your sister think when Leila turned up in your life? You couldn't have lost your mother long? You must have been grieving terribly?"

"Miranda, we're not talking about *me*," he told her curtly, shaken by her perception. "We're talking about you."

"So *you* say!" she responded, undeterred. "Where did I get my brains from anyway? My maths gene, for a start. I was always very good at maths. My grandparents were lovely people. Full of good practical common sense. My grandfather could fix any piece of machinery on the farm. My grandmother was a great cook and a great dressmaker. But they wouldn't have called themselves intellectuals. Neither of them read much."

"Of course you *are* an intellectual," he said, not sparing the dry-as-bone tone.

"No need to be sarcastic. I *am*. Fact of life, and I don't take the credit. I inherited what brain I have from the boy—the man—who was my father. Leila can't be too bright if she didn't think I was going to track her down one day."

"But there's no way you want to meet her?" He trapped her gaze. God, wouldn't that be an event to be in on?

"What? Show up unannounced? No way! I might tackle her to the ground and start pummelling her. Not that I've ever done anything like that before."

"Miranda, don't underestimate the woman you say is your mother," he rasped. "It's far more likely she'd seize you by the hair and have you thrown out. That's if you could get *in*. My stepmother isn't your normal woman."

"Now, isn't that exactly what I've been telling you?" she cried, her turquoise-green eyes opened wide. "She's a *cruel* person. She broke her loving parents' hearts. My grandmother died without her only child by her side. I don't really care that Leila didn't want *me*. Who the heck do I look like anyway?" She tugged in frustration at a loose silver-gilt curl. "What's with the hair? The colour of my eyes? There's my father out there somewhere. I might go looking for him. Did he even know about me? Actually, I've got a few doubts about *your* father. Given he's the big mining magnate, how come he fell for Leila hook, line and sinker? What got into him?"

"Let's not go there, Miranda," he said tersely.

"Okay, she's beautiful. She's gorgeous. And she must be great in bed."

And as dangerous as a taipan. "Are you done?" he asked, amazed. This seventeen-year-old girl was a total stranger, yet already they had made a strong connection.

"Don't get angry with me, Corin," she urged gently. "I could be worse. I could be out to make trouble, but I'm not. I don't want to stress this—it's a bit embarrassing—but look at the big picture. Aren't we related by marriage?"

"I only have your word for it," he answered, very sharply

indeed because he was rattled. "Plus a few old photographs as some sort of proof."

"Please…I don't want you to be angry and upset. You might be keeping it well under wraps, but I think you have…difficulties in life."

He didn't care he sounded so cutting. "You're a very special person, Miranda." She had to be. Every cell in his body was drawn to her. It was an involuntary reaction. But sometimes one had to be cruel to be kind.

"You believe me, though, don't you?" The glitter of unshed tears was back in her eyes at his harshness. "You believe *me* more than you would believe the woman you've known for years. I bet she's been no friend to your sister. You *do* love your sister?"

He gritted his teeth. "Do you expect me to sit still for this interrogation?"

"Okay, okay!" She pressed her hands together as though in prayer. "I shouldn't have said it. Let's get back to what I need to get me through med school. I promise I'll work harder than I ever have in my life. Back me and I won't let you down. I'll even try to pay you back once I qualify."

He was driven to dropping his head into his hands. "Miranda, just stop talking for a moment. I'm going to check out your whole story. Or have my people do it for me. Don't worry. They're professionals. It will all be very confidential. None of the information they supply to me will get out. Where is this flat of yours?"

She was so nervous, excited, upset, her hands were shaking. "Look, I'll write it down for you. And my mobile number. I hope I didn't seriously ruin your day?"

"I can't pretend you haven't stunned me." He shot back his cuff to check his watch. "I have a very tedious dinner party tonight I can't get out of. I'll get Gil to drop me off first at my apartment, then he can take you home."

She became agitated. "No, no, don't bother. I don't want to put you to the trouble. Besides, I can't possibly arrive back at the flat in a Rolls."

"Gil can stop and let you out a short distance away," he said shortly. "Anyway, it will be dark by the time he gets there." He lifted his hand to signal the chauffeur, who now turned their way, walking down the path.

"So, will you let me know?" In her agitation she reached out to grip his hand hard, feeling the little shock wave of skin on skin. "Can I trust you, Corin? I *do* need help."

"Have you told anyone else about this? Your friends?"

The brilliant gaze seared her. "Gosh, no! I promise you I haven't told a living soul."

"A smart move, Miranda, for a smart girl. You'll hear from me within a few days. We'll do this thing legitimately."

"Legitimately, how?" She perked up.

"I'll tell you when I judge it time for you to know," he said dismissively. "But if you've dreamed up some story—"

"Then you're free to go to the police." She spoke with intensity. "It's no story, Corin. That's why you've been giving me a hearing. Even if your stepmother did lay eyes on me she wouldn't recognise me."

"On the other hand she might," he answered her bluntly. "There is such a thing as genetics. You said it yourself. How did Leila produce a child with silver-gilt hair and turquoise-green eyes? It has to be your father's legacy."

"Or it could be any number of complex interactions." She frowned in concentration. "So many variables—enzyms, proteins, biological phenomenon. I'm greatly interested in genetics and genomics, molecular biology. Why wouldn't I be? I don't even know who I am. That should put me at a serious disadvantage psychologically."

He saw humour in that. "I don't think so, Miranda. You appear pretty well integrated to me."

"Gee, thanks!" She flushed with genuine pleasure. His good opinion meant a great deal. "Trust me, Corin," she said earnestly. "Leila has totally forgotten she ever had a child."

He swallowed his caustic retort. Hadn't Zara always said there would come a time Leila, their stepmother, the central figure in their father's life, would be caught out?

And so it began.

CHAPTER ONE

The present.

THE top floor of the immense glass-and-steel monolith, the command post of Rylance Metals, housed the multibillion-dollar corporation's hierarchy. As Miranda rode the elevator to Corin's office she had an overwhelming feeling she shouldn't be in this building. Not that she would have to duck if she saw anyone. She had been inside Rylance Tower on isolated occasions over the past three years and no one had taken the slightest notice of her. Why would they? Her status of university student would have been obvious to them from her classic student dress. Besides, the Rylance Foundation sponsored a number of gifted students. They came and went. On those occasions she had been careful to maintain her camouflage. On campus she was a lot more flamboyant. Some of her girlfriends laughingly called her a *fashionista*. Amazing what one could do on a low budget, given a bit of flair. She had inherited that flair from someone. Leila? Leila was renowned for her style.

She had long since learned from Corin that Leila had been given a position on the board by her besotted husband. Corin had become so important to her she could recognise the fact he deplored his father's decision. Not that he spoke about it. Only once, and then briefly. Corin played his cards very close to his chest. Mercifully today there was no chance of running into the woman who had abandoned her soon after birth. Leila only ventured into Rylance Tower for board meetings. Right now, she and her husband, Dalton Rylance, were in Singapore—a mix of business and pleasure, the newspapers said. Corin said *business*. It was always *business*. But Leila would get the opportunity to spend lots of money to make up for the time she had to spend on her own and so prevent herself from getting bored.

As Miranda stepped out into the hushed corridor, thickly carpeted and lined with architectural drawings—the corporation had its own architectural as well as engineering departments—she checked her watch. Ten minutes until Corin would see her. She was always early, never late for Corin. It was pleasant to make a little light conversation with his secretary, the beautifully groomed, forty-something Clare Howard, who was devoted to him and exceptionally good at her job. As she would have to be.

Afterwards, Miranda took a seat on one of the sofas facing a granite-and-chrome coffee table neatly stacked with trade magazines and financial papers. She picked up one, flipping through it without actually seeing anything. Today she had allowed herself a little more pizzazz with her dress. Ms Howard had kindly made a comment on how lovely she looked. Her dress *was* pretty. The yellow silk background was splashed with tiny daisy-like flowers in deep blue, violet and turquoise, with a fine tracery of green leaves. A sale coup. All the major department stores were running them in the recession. New turquoise sandals and a turquoise tote bag that looked a whole lot more expensive than they were completed the outfit. Her hair she continued to wear short, cutting her bubble of curls herself, sometimes enlisting a girlfriend's help for the back of her head. She didn't have the time or the money to go all-out with a glamorous new hairstyle. She had maintained her part-time job—waitressing at city restaurants, three nights a week—but that money was stretched to the limit. She had been given assistance by the Rylance Foundation to rent her inner-city flat, which was in a good, safe, very convenient area.

With two minutes to go she could feel the rise in her blood pressure. One's blood pressure always rose when in the company of someone one was attracted to. Fact. She ached over her reasons. At least she felt confident she looked good. Healthy, eyes bright, skin glowing, despite the endless hours of burning the midnight oil.

Over the past three years she had grown close to Corin. She told herself it was in a quasi *professional* way. Mentor-protégée sort of thing. He always appeared pleased to see her at any rate, and was always willing to take the time to listen to her accounts of student life. A friendship had been established, but they both took good care to keep within the proper framework. Wealth could open doors for people. Corin had opened a door for her. She was immensely grateful. So much so she had gone all out to top her graduating class. Corin had actually taken the time to attend, clapping enthusiastically after she had given her speech.

"I knew the moment I laid eyes on you, you were a girl with enormous potential." This with a mocking sparkle in his dark eyes.

By now she knew his every expression, every nuance of his resonant voice. She knew she had to be extremely careful to control her feelings. Her career was mapped out. She had to concentrate on her studies. She couldn't allow emotion to get in the way. A show of emotion—however slight—could jeopardise her standing with Corin. There was a definite etiquette involved. She could not overstep the mark. Fortunately she had mastered the art of masking her deepest feelings. She might not appear vulnerable. But vulnerable she was. Privately she had run out of making excuses for herself. The truth was she had a huge crush on Corin Rylance.

Get real! You're madly in love with him.

No one must ever know.

They shared their dark secret about Leila, but they rarely allowed it to come to the surface. From time to time she weakened in her discipline, always when she was in bed at night, allowing herself to wonder what Corin was doing. Who he was doing it with. Lately there had been rumours of an impending engagement that made the muscles of her stomach clench at every mention. Corin—married! Yet it seemed to her Corin didn't have the look of a man in love. The young woman in the spotlight was one of his circle. Annette Atwood. An extremely attractive brunette of imposing height, with a great figure. A real figure. Naturally Ms Atwood was asked everywhere. Photographed wherever she went. Lately the paparazzi had taken to following her as though they *knew* she was a strong contender to become the heir apparent's wife. Corin himself never spoke of her. But then, since she had met him Corin hadn't spoken of any particular woman. Except his sister, Zara, who was working in London at a big financial institution. Zara had a Masters in Business. She had an excellent head on her shoulders and was also very artistic, like their mother and her side of the family. Zara was a gifted artist, but their father had been totally against her trying to make a career as a painter.

"A hobby, girl. Just a hobby! Live in the real world. Can't abide dabblers."

The image Miranda kept getting was that Dalton Rylance wasn't a nice man at all. No comfort to his children—especially his daughter. No wonder Dalton and her mother were inseparable. They were creatures of the jungle. Power was all that counted.

"Hi, Miranda!" Corin looked up from something he had been reading to give her his irresistible smile. It was impossible not to smile back. "Take a seat, won't you?" He gestured towards the leather armchairs arranged companionably on the opposite side of his desk. It was a huge space, his office, beautifully and comfortably furnished. Hundreds of leather-bound volumes gleamed through the antique English mahogany cabinets. A neat pile of files sat to one side on his desk; one was open before him. No disorder whatever. Everything in its proper place. There was a splendid view over the city towers and the broad, deep river to his back. "Clare is organising coffee. We have a few things we need to discuss."

"Oh, Corin, like what?" She was feeling a little giddy at the sight of him—he looked so vibrant, impossible not to stare—so she quickly took an armchair opposite, folding her hands with a commendable show of calm in her lap.

"You look well," he sidetracked. In fact, she looked enchanting. He had never seen her in so pretty or so feminine a dress. She was such an intriguing combination of inner strength and physical delicacy. No doubt she had picked the dress to suit her rare colouring. She probably knew her eyes were the exact colour of the turquoise flowers. He wanted to tell her. Thought he'd better not. Miranda kept her own space.

"So do you." She stared back at him with a little worried

frown. "Why is it I think you're about to persuade me to take a gap year?" He had raised the subject before, but had since let it drop. She should have known better.

"Well, it *is* a good idea," he said mildly.

She glanced away. A large canvas hung on the far wall. It depicted a lush rainforest scene with the buttressed trunk of a giant tree of extraordinary shape in the foreground. The magnificent tree was surrounded by a wide circle of copper-coloured dry leaves, and ferns of all kinds, fungi and terrestrial white orchids sprouted everywhere in the background. His sister, Zara, had painted it. Miranda, who had a good eye for such things, loved it. The scene looked so real—so immediate—one could almost walk into it. "I can handle the studying, Corin." She looked back slowly.

He held up an elegant, long-fingered hand. "Please, Miranda, don't look so crestfallen."

"How can I not be?"

"You push yourself too hard. I worry about you."

"You worry about me?" Her heart gave a quick jolt.

"Why look so surprised?"

"You don't *have* to," she said, trying to hide her immense gratification. He *worried* about her?

"Of course I do," he confirmed. "You're virtually an orphan. We share a history."

She didn't say she worried about *him* when he went off on his field trips to inspect various corporation mine sites.

With every passing year he had become more handsome and compelling. She watched with a mix of fascination and trepidation as he stood up, then came around his desk to perch on the edge of it. He was always impeccably dressed. Beautiful suits, shirts, ties, cufflinks, supple expensive shoes. The lot! How could she not fall in love with a man like that?

"I know you can handle the mind-numbing workload," he said. "You've demonstrated ample proof of that. But you're still very young, Miranda. Only twenty. Not twenty-one until next June, which is months off. I don't want you totally blitzed."

She drew in a long breath, preparing to argue. "Corin—"

Again he chopped her off with a gesture of his hand. "A gap year would give you time for personal development. Time to develop your other skills. You need to get a balance in life, Miranda. Believe me, it will all help in your chosen profession. You could travel. See something of the world. Do research if you like."

She couldn't hold back her derision. "Travel? You must be joking."

"Do I look like I'm joking?" He lifted a black brow. "I'm very serious about this, Miranda. You're not just another brilliant student we're sponsoring. The two of us have a strong connection. Your mother is married to my father. Many people thought it would be all over within a year or two, but they were wrong. She knows *exactly* how to handle him."

"It has to be sex," she said with a dark frown. "Razzle-dazzle." Leila Rylance was famous for her beauty and glamour, her parties. From all accounts she had made herself knowledgeable about the political and big business scene. Even the art world, where she was fêted by gallery-owners. Leila was right at the top of the tree when it came to social-climbers.

"Don't knock it," Corin was saying dryly. "It's important. Dad is still a vigorous and virile man. Besides, Leila has numerous other wiles at her disposal. She runs his private life and the house—indeed the houses all over the world—with considerable competence. She's no fool. She's appears very loving, very loyal, very respectful. She hangs on my father's every word."

"But is it for real?" Miranda demanded with a good deal of fire. "She obviously didn't win you and Zara over."

There was a flash in his brilliant dark eyes. "He brought her frequently to the house before our mother died, like she was a colleague and not an employee well down the rung. Fooled no one. At one stage I thought our housekeeper Matty was planning on poisoning her over morning tea. Matty adored our mother. Leila spent a lot of time trying to charm us. We were only children, but *thinking* children. We could see she posed a real threat to our parents' marriage. Dad lusted after Leila long before she got him to marry her."

She studied his handsome, brooding face, seeing how it must have been for him and his sister. "So hurting people didn't concern her? Between the two of them they must have broken your mother's heart."

His expression was grim. "It was pretty harrowing for all of us. My beautiful mother most of all. I can't talk about it, Miranda. I'll never forgive either of them."

"Why would you? I'd feel exactly the same. I *do* feel the same. The thing is, do they *know*? Does your father know? You're his heir."

He gave a brief laugh. "My grandparents, the De Laceys, are major shareholders. My grandfather Hugo still sits on the board. It was he who staked my father in the beginning—a lot of money, I can tell you. I have my mother's shares. And Zara and I will have our grandparents' eventually. Dad couldn't overthrow me even if he wanted to. Which he doesn't. In his own peculiar way he's proud of me. It's Zara, my beautiful, gifted sister, he endeavours to avoid. I look like *him*, except his eyes are a piercing pale blue and mine are dark."

"They're beautiful eyes," she said without thinking.

"Thank you." He smiled, thus lightening the atmosphere.

"But I still say yours are the most remarkable eyes I've ever seen."

"Someone has them," she said. "My biological father? Some member of his family? Even you with all your resources couldn't find out who my father was."

"We couldn't, and Lord knows my people tried. But we don't know if it's a good or a bad thing. Some people don't want to become involved—not many years after, when the pattern of their lives is set. No one in the area where your grandparents and Leila lived fitted the bill or the time frame. It could have been someone she just happened to meet—"

"Like a one-night stand?" Miranda said sharply. "Barely sixteen, and Leila was taking lovers? Or was she raped? I can't bear to think about that." She shuddered. "My grandmother was convinced from the way Leila acted and spoke that wasn't the case."

Corin's eyes never left her face. "There's no way to tell, Miranda. I'm sorry. Only Leila knows. One day you might get the opportunity to ask her—" He broke off at a discreet tap on the door, calling for entry. A young woman Miranda had never seen before wheeled a trolley into the office.

"Thank you, Fiona. We'll take it from here."

"Yes, Mr Rylance." Fiona flashed him her most dazzling smile, at the same time managing to give Miranda a comprehensive once-over.

Fiona left. Miranda stood up. "I'll pour. No milk? Teaspoon of sugar?" She remembered.

"Fine." His mind was clearly focused on something else.

"Want one of these sandwiches and a Danish?"

"Why not?" He went back to sit at his desk.

They were both settled before he spoke again. "This coffee is good."

"Nothing less than the best." It *was* very good. So were the neat little chicken sandwiches and the freshly baked mini-pastries. She was hungry. She'd only had fruit for breakfast. Papaya with a spritz of lime.

"Money would be made available for you to travel," Corin said, setting down his coffee cup.

She looked at him in amazement. "You can't be serious, Corin! Why would you do that? I'm taking enough. Can I say no?"

His brilliant eyes burned into her. "Better to say yes, Miranda."

"Oh, Lord!" She took another hasty swallow of the excellent coffee. "You're worried about burn-out. Is that it?"

"There *is* such a thing. We both know that. The sheer drudgery of study. Your friend Peter almost died from an overdose."

Her head sank. "Poor Peter!" Peter—her friend, the brilliant class geek. She had looked out for him from the start. When other students had tended to mock his extreme shyness and his bone-thin appearance she had been his constant support. Peter's appearance at that stage of his life hadn't matched up with his formidable brain.

"You were devastated," Corin reminded her. Did she *know* poor Peter idolised her?

"Of course I was devastated," she said, lifting her head. "We were supposed to be friends, but he never *told* me how bad he felt. Why didn't he? I could have helped."

"You can't blame yourself, Miranda. You were a good friend to Peter, but his depression got the better of him. He was the classic square peg in a round hole."

"Wasn't he just?" She sighed. "I'm so grateful you were there for me that night." Not knowing what else to do, she had called Corin from the hospital and he had come. "I'll always remember that. And what you did for Peter afterwards. You spoke to his family. They listened. They'd been blind to the fact Peter wasn't meant to be a doctor. With the family medical background they more or less forced him into it. Peter desperately wanted to become a musician. His ambition wasn't taken at all seriously until you spoke up."

"I wanted to help."

"Well, you did." These days Peter was studying the cello at the very prestigeous Royal College of Music in London.

"Still hearing from him?" Corin asked.

"All the time."

She smiled. A sweet, uncomplicated smile. Peter was her friend. No more. He would never be her lover. He was glad about that. He didn't stop to question why. But emotions had such intrusive, pressing qualities. Sometimes they had to be pushed away.

"I love Zara's rainforest painting," she said, gesturing to it.

"So do I. Zara keeps up her painting. I'll find one of hers for you. I have quite a collection. But we're not talking about Zara. Or Peter—though I'm very glad to hear he's doing so well. We're talking about *you*, Miranda. I firmly believe you'll benefit from a gap year."

Her fingers laced themselves together.

"Don't argue. You wanted to fast-track science, remember?"

She looked across at him with pleading eyes. "I could have done it in two years had I worked through the long vacations."

His tongue clicked with impatience. "Why won't you admit you were *glad* when I made the decision for you? I'm on your side, Miranda. I'm simply not going to allow you to crash and burn. Two years was far too gruelling for a three-year science course and you know it. No time at all for a personal life."

"Who needs a personal life?" she asked discordantly, stretching her slender arms along the sides of the armchair. "*You're* a workaholic, though rumour has it you're going to marry Annette Atwood. She's stunning."

He let the silence build. "So she is," he agreed eventually. "But you appear to know more about it than I do."

"You're *not*?" It came out far too intensely. Damn, damn, *damn*.

"Let's get back to you," he said smoothly, aware she hadn't meant to show such interest. "Professor Sutton shares my view you'd benefit from a gap year. And *there's* a man who thinks the world of you."

Her expression softened. "The Prof would like me to stick to science. He's told me many times. He thinks I have a future in medical research. When you think about it, nine of our ten Nobel Prize winners have been medical scientists, or doctors of medicine. And Patrick White, of course, for Literature. I know at some future stage the Prof would like me to be in a position to make his team. I'm sure he's told you he's enormously grateful for the funding he receives from the Foundation?"

"He's doing great work," Corin acknowledged, as though that said it all. "Research doesn't appeal to you?"

She ran her fingers through her short glittering curls. "I'd be honoured. But I have to get my MB first, Corin." Her brain was ticking over at a million miles a minute. Travel? See the world? She felt exhilarated. And shocked.

"No reason to believe you won't. I applaud your ambition. But taking a gap year will work out to be a distinct advantage. The more experienced and the more cultivated you are as a human being, you can only enhance your chosen career."

"So I'm to do what I'm told? Is that it?"

He could see the mix of emotions in her eyes. "I've mapped out an agenda for your perusal."

"Not my approval?" she commented wryly.

He ignored that. "Zara will be happy to keep an eye on you in London. I know the two of you will get on like a house on fire. Dad splashed out and bought a house in London when our mother was alive—an 1840s house in Holland Park. Rather run-down at the time, but in a superb location of beautiful tree-lined streets and gardens, and of course the park itself, which was once the grounds of a vast Jacobean Manor. Anyway, my mother and her English decorator transformed it. Zara is living in the house now. But there's a basement apartment which I had turned into a very comfortable *pied-à-terre* for whenever I'm in London. You could live there. It will give you the feeling of independence. You can come and go as you please, but Zara would still be around for you. There's a very elegant apartment in Paris too, typically Parisian, but Leila doesn't go there often. She much prefers the villa she talked Dad into buying on the Côte d'Azur. It has a spectacular view of the Mediterranean."

"So in the years of her marriage Leila has lived like royalty, greedily soaking up all the luxury your father's billions can buy?"

"It's not a new phenomenon. There have always been courtesans."

"You hate her, don't you?"

"I hate what she did to my *mother*," he said tautly. "And how shamelessly. That's when it all began. She worked to alienate Zara from Dad. These days I'm…indifferent to her."

Miranda had to wonder about that. Only eight years separated Corin and Leila. "She must have to work very hard to be indifferent to *you*!" She spoke without thinking.

His handsome face tightened and his whole body tensed. "What's that supposed to mean?"

She reined herself in quickly. "Leila likes to charm wherever she goes. Men, that is."

"Well, she doesn't charm *me*!" His voice was heavily freighted with hostility.

"Okay, don't be angry."

"Maybe you should start thinking about psychiatry?"

She met his dark eyes. "You've said that before. I've got good instincts, Corin. I let them work for me. Are you going to show me that agenda of yours?"

"I've got it right here." He picked up a sheet of paper, then passed it across the desk to her. He must have been checking it when she arrived. "A bank account will be opened for you. You'll have all the money you need to travel. See the great art museums of the world, study a language if you like. Go to the opera, the theatre, the ballet. Zara loves the ballet. Buy clothes. I want you to make the best of this time, Miranda. You'll have a long, hard slog ahead of you."

Her eyes ran dazedly down the page. "Look, I can't do this, Corin," she said eventually. "I'm not family. Yet you're treating me like family."

"Oh, for God's sake, you *are* family—in a way. Your mother is married to my father. That's family. Besides, I'm fond of you, Miranda. You must know that. We clicked from the very first moment you near landed in my lap. Your welfare has become important. It's the least I can do for someone who has taken more than her share of blows. We're both caught up in this, Miranda, so you *must* do as I say. This gap year will work wonders. Just see how quickly it goes."

She closed her eyes briefly. "So a girl's gotta do what a girl's gotta do? Is that it?"

"I want your promise right now," he said.

Her eyes opened. Her head flew back. "What if Leila and your father decide to visit London, or the Paris apartment or whatever?" she queried with sharp concern. "I see there's another apartment in Rome."

"You wouldn't need to have contact should they visit. Leila likes the great hotels. Claridges in London, the Ritz in Paris are favourites. Dad does what she wants. She's an expert manipulator. Anyway, I'll always know their movements. Leave it to me."

"Leave it to you?" She drew in a stunned breath. "I'm shocked by all this, Corin. I knew you might spring the gap year on me again, but never an agenda like this! Zara still doesn't know about me and Leila?"

"I don't think she could handle it," he said sombrely. "Not without speaking out. She knows about my clever protégée Miranda Thornton. She knows nothing about the family connection. It'll have to wait."

"Until you're good and ready, Machiavelli. Do protégées usually get world trips and a hefty bank allowance?"

"My sister knows I have a reason for everything I do," he answered smoothly. "She won't question it, or you. All she needs to know is that I consider, as does Professor Sutton, you'll gain a great deal from a gap year."

Her beautiful eyes glittered like jewels. "I think I knew from the start it might end up like this. You changing my life."

His mouth twisted sardonically. "Cheer up! Didn't you once call it destiny?"

"You believe in it?"

Their eyes locked. For the longest moment. "I do," he said.

CHAPTER TWO

IT WAS more like a fairy tale than real life. She was living a glittering lifestyle, like the most impossible of dreams. She had to remind herself every day that she couldn't allow such a life to seduce her. Not that there was any real chance of that. Zara was the heiress. She most assuredly wasn't. The practice of medicine would be *her* role in life. But for now she was enjoying herself immensely—just as Corin had wanted her to. Days, weeks, months simply flew by in a whirl of pleasure and excitement. She was learning a new way of life, acquiring much knowledge along the way.

She loved London—perhaps not the climate, not after the blue and gold of Queensland, but she worked around that like everyone else. London was one of the great cities of the world. It embraced her. It allowed her to trace its illustrious history, to see its magnificent historic buildings, the art galleries, the wonderful antiques shops, markets, to shop at the legendary Harrods, visit the beautiful parks. She was doubly blessed by being billeted in very swish Holland Park, just west of Notting Hill. More than anything she loved living in Corin's elegant apartment, with its French Art Deco furniture and a basic colour scheme of brown, bronze and white enlivened by cinnamon and gold. It was definitely a male sanctum, but it welcomed her.

Though fourteen thousand miles separated them, she somehow felt Corin very close. That could have had a lot to do with the fact that she was sleeping in *his* huge Art Deco bed!

Zara was largely responsible for the lovely time she was having. She had quickly found Zara was the most beautiful, gracious creature on earth. And the kindest. A true lady. Miranda knew from the photographs of their mother—Corin had one lovely silver framed study he kept on his desk—Zara was fashioned in her mother's image, but she did see a lot of Corin in her. The sharpness of intellect, the generosity of spirit, the sense of humour that happily they all shared. Just like Corin, there was something utterly irresistible about Zara. Yet Miranda sensed a deep sadness that lay in Zara's heart. From time to time it was reflected in her huge dark eyes. Zara had some pretty serious stuff stacked away in the background.

Over the months Zara had taken the place of the big sister Miranda had never had. She had been so lonely for siblings that had never arrived. How could they? Her real mother, Leila, had fled, desperate to get away from her parents and her child. She now claimed she couldn't bear children. Maybe, just maybe, it was true. Leila would surely have wanted to cement her new position by producing a male child? It was possible it was Dalton Rylance who didn't want or need any more children. He had Corin and his daughter, even if she so painfully brought to mind his first wife. Was his cold disregard a by-product of his guilt? Miranda found herself both fascinated and repelled by the whole story.

Kathryn Rylance had died when she'd crashed her car. Had it been an accident? She would never dare ask. But surely such a loving mother would never have deliberately left her children? Not to such a father. Or the covetous young woman waiting in the wings. The potential stepmother. There could have been a single moment when Kathryn had become careless and lost control of the wheel. She could have been blinded by tears. Miranda realised she wouldn't be the only one to ponder such things. There were the grieving grandparents, the De Laceys, and Kathryn's clever, perceptive children, her close friends. Talk must have been rife!

But no one knew what really happened. Nor would they ever.

Often she wanted to break her own silence and confide in Zara, but she had given her promise to Corin. *He* would decide when it was time. In the meantime, Zara was always on hand with support and advice. She took Miranda everywhere—parties, functions, art showings—and introduced her to many highly placed people who seemed to like her. She was now included in many invitations. Zara arranged weekend trips to Paris, the fabulous City of Light, where they crammed in as much sightseeing as they could. All for her benefit, of course. Zara had visited the city many times before.

Back in London they lunched together whenever Zara could make it from work, went shopping together, loving every moment of it. But Zara never interfered or asked too many questions. It was as if she knew Miranda wasn't too sure of the answers. The great thing was they had become the best of friends. Miranda valued that friendship greatly. For a young woman with a billionaire father Zara was remarkably down to earth. But Miranda, acutely attuned to Corin and now to his sister, knew Zara wasn't happy at heart. It wasn't as if she brooded or was subject to mood swings, nothing like that, but Miranda felt right in her judgement. Beautiful, privileged Zara, for all the money behind her and a long list of admirers, wasn't happy or fulfilled. A melancholy lay behind the melting dark eyes that those who looked beyond the superficial clearly saw.

Miranda had written to Peter well in advance of her arrival. He had been thrilled to know she was coming. He thoroughly agreed with Corin, whom he referred to as his saviour, a gap year was an excellent idea.

"You don't want to end up a burnt-out old wreck like me."

These days they met up frequently for coffee and conversation, took in a concert or a movie. On good days, like today, when the sun was shining, they packed a picnic lunch and sat on the grass in either Hyde Park or St James's, with its wonderful views of Buckingham Palace in one direction and Whitehall in the other. There was just so much history to this great city! Currently Peter's teacher had entered him in a big European competition and convinced Peter if he worked hard and continued to show progress he would make his mark in the world of music.

"You're in your element at last, aren't you?" Miranda said, glancing over at her friend with affection. Peter had made a complete recovery now that he had been granted his wish to pursue a musical career.

"Absolutely!" Peter lolled on the green grass, tucking into a ham and salad roll. "I've never felt so at home in my life. I love London. All the action is here. And there's no culture gap to contend with. Even the family has settled, knowing I'm making a success of myself over here. Life's strange, isn't it? I wouldn't be here except for Corin. My parents actually listened to him. But then he has enormous presence and—what?—he's not even thirty."

"Twenty-eight." Miranda took the last bite out of her crunchy apple.

"Still in love with him?" Peter leaned on an elbow to peer into her face.

"Why ever would you say that?" She feigned nonchalance though her heart had started to hammer. Was she that transparent?

"Come off it, Miri," he scoffed gently. "I'm super-observant when it comes to you. Heck, I don't blame you. I could fall in love with him myself and I'm not gay. Corin has more going for him than the law should allow. It's a wonder some determined young woman hasn't snaffled him up."

Carefully Miranda wiped her hands, putting the apple core into a disposable bag. "There *is* one determined young woman on the scene. But no announcements as yet. Annette Atwood. You know the family?"

"Of course!" Peter nodded. His best feature, his mane of thick golden-brown hair, gleamed in the sun. He was growing it artistically long, as Miranda had suggested. The look suited him and added a certain panache. "Dad's a big-time lawyer turned property developer?"

"That's the one."

"Think they'll make a go of it?" Peter asked, sensitive to how Miranda might feel about that.

"Corin has never come close to telling me about his love life," Miranda returned very dryly.

"What about *your* love life?" He turned questioning blue eyes on her. Corin's sister, who was a really lovely person and a great beauty in the classic style, was making it her business to introduce Miri to a lot of high-flying guys.

But Miranda smiled as though she didn't have a care in the world. "I have a powerful reason to stay on course, Peter. So do you. We have careers lined up."

"That we do. I've often wondered where your driving

interest in medicine and medical research came from, Miri. Your background isn't like mine, with so many doctors in it. They say genius is random. Dad says it has to be in your genes."

"Then it must be a very long way back." She laughed. "I come from a line of small farmers."

"So it's just as they say. Genius is random."

"And we're *both* geniuses!" She lightly punched his arm. "Better get going. Haven't you got a master class at three-thirty?"

Peter started. "Hell, I almost forget. It's so lovely being with you, Miri." He stood up, all of six-four, dusting his jeans off. "So, what are you going to do about your birthday? It's coming up. I suppose Zara will have something arranged?"

"No, no!" She shook her head vigorously. "Zara doesn't know anything about it. And you are *not* to tell her. I don't want any fuss. No presents, except a little one from my best mate—and that's you!"

"But you *should* celebrate!" he insisted. "You're only twenty-one once."

"It's no big deal."

"Of course it is! What say we get dressed up and have dinner at some posh hotel? I have money. The parents are very generous these days."

Miranda handed over the picnic basket, then took his arm. "That will suit me just fine."

Peter felt so happy he could have shouted with joy.

The best laid plans could always go awry, and circumstance forced them to move her birthday date forward to mid-week. Peter had been selected at short notice to replace the cellist in a highly regarded quartet, who had fallen ill. With a new member on board, intensive rehearsals would have to take place all over the weekend.

"No worries, Peter," she reassured him, thrilled he was getting such a lucky break. "New horizons are opening up for you. Wednesday evening will be fine."

And so it eventually turned out that Miranda's early twenty-first birthday dinner with the young man who would become her life-long friend proved a special treat.

The following day Zara and three of her colleagues, all foreign-exchange traders, led by her boss, Sir Marcus Boyle, were to fly off to Berlin for a series of top-level business meetings.

Zara eased her tall, elegant body into the jacket of her Armani suit, picked up her briefcase, then walked to the front door that led onto its own private patch of emerald-green lawn and blossoming flowerbeds. Miranda was holding the door open for her, waving acknowledgement to the London taxi driver who had just arrived to take Zara to Heathrow. At twenty-six, Zara was very good indeed at her job. Miranda had learned that from one of her colleagues at a recent party.

"Tremendous flair. Not afraid of taking risks. She's a star turn. In the genes, I suppose, as a Rylance. Rival banks regularly try to lure our Zara away. So far no luck!"

"I'll be back Tuesday." Zara smiled at the girl she had come to regard as the nearest thing she would ever have to a younger sister. "Be good. Don't accept any solo invitations from Eddie Walton. He's really keen on you, but he's too old and too much the playboy. As I told you, he was involved in a rather high-profile scandal not all that long back. Likes the ladies, does our Viscount Edward."

"Don't worry, I can look after myself," Miranda assured her. "Besides, I'm immune to Eddie's mature charms. Though he does have them."

"That he does," Zara agreed wryly. "Well, look after yourself, Miri." Zara bent to give the petite Miranda a real kiss on the cheek. "You don't mind watering the plants, do you? There are rather a lot of them."

"It'll be a pleasure."

"Thank you," Zara said gratefully. "Oh, yes, that reminds me. You're set for the charity do Wednesday evening?"

"Looking forward to it." Miranda gave Zara a final hug. "Go on, now. The taxi is waiting. Have a safe trip and wow them in Berlin."

Zara's answer came in a fluent flow of German that sounded perfect to Miranda's ears. She continued to stand on the doorstep of the handsome pristine white terrace house, watching until the taxi had disappeared.

You'll be alone, all alone, on your twenty-first birthday, girl.

Not that she minded being alone—she was fully aware how blessed she was being taken on by Corin and Zara—but it was her twenty-first birthday after all. She hadn't dared tell Zara about it. Zara would have done her utmost to organise something—even try to get out of the scheduled Berlin meetings.

With a little sigh, she shut the glass door of the big beautiful house and leaned against it.

Be happy, Miranda. It's not so terrible, is it, to be alone on your birthday?

Of a sudden her eyes filled with emotional tears. She blinked them back, feeling ashamed of herself. She had been handed a marvellous London sojourn on a plate. Trips to Paris. A luxurious lifestyle. The ease and affection of Zara's company. Most young women could only dream of being offered such an experience.

Buck up!

She breathed deeply. Corin knew it was her birthday

tomorrow. No card had arrived. Maybe he thought a card might have alerted Zara? Flowers perhaps tomorrow? A possibility. She made a real effort to brighten up, wondering if she would ever find anyone in the world to fall in love with after Corin Rylance.

It was after midnight before she finished reading the latest novel by a writer she always enjoyed, Laura Lippman. She set the book down on the bedside table before turning off the light. The beautifully laundered sheets and pillowcases had a lovely fragrance of mimosa. Zara would have asked for it especially, as a reminder of home. Mimosa, or wattle to Australians, the national flower.

With practice Miranda had mastered the knack of putting herself into some lovely serene place to enable her to drift off to sleep. These places were always near water—the ocean, a lake, a river—with lots of blue and gold, a background of leafy trees, spring green…

She didn't know how long she had been asleep, but she awoke with a great start and a swiftly muffled cry of fright in her throat. There were movements—soft, muted sounds—coming from upstairs in the house. She sat up, straining her ears, while the atmosphere in the apartment settled like a heavy blanket around her. She knew perfectly well she had set the state-of-the-art security system just as Zara had shown her. Who or what could have de-activated it? Should she ring the security people? Hastily she turned on a bedside lamp, checking the time: *1:30 a.m.* She had never been more aware of how exposed a lone woman could be. She said a quick prayer—not at all convinced there was really someone up there to hear her, but prepared to give it a shot.

Stacks of valuable things were in the house. Paintings,

antiques, silver, Oriental porcelain, rugs. Heart thudding, she slid out of bed, pulling on the turquoise silk kimono Zara had insisted on buying for her.

"It exactly matches your eyes, Miri. You must have it!"

She took several deep breaths. Held them. An exercise in slowing her heart-rate. Then very quietly she let herself out of the apartment into the staircase hall that connected the apartment to the house proper. For the first time since arriving in London she felt very much alone. The area lay in intense darkness. She reached out her fingers, seeking the bank of switches. She pressed one and a single low-level light came on, gleaming against the teal-blue-painted wall with its collection of miniatures in gilded frames. Now she could find her way up the curving internal staircase. A good twenty-four oak steps. Before leaving the apartment she had taken the precaution of arming herself with one of Corin's golf clubs, which for some reason she had kept handy: an iron, a lethal weapon. God forbid she would have to use it. Maybe wave it about threateningly. Her mobile was in the pocket of her embroidered silk robe. She could ring the police.

Why don't you do it now?

What if it's Leila with Corin's father?

She very nearly went into a panic at the idea. Surely Zara would have told her of their impending arrival in London?

That was if Zara even knew they were coming.

A whole world of problems opened up. Corin had been adamant Leila favoured the great hotels of the world when she was traveling, even though her husband maintained residences in various capital cities. Besides, Zara was in residence, and there was no love lost between Zara, her father and his second wife. None of them would have wanted to come into contact.

What a dysfunctional family! Leila the stepmother was at

the root of it all. Leila, her birth mother. She had a hard time with that. If Leila ever laid eyes on her what reaction would she get? She had to closely resemble *someone*, in her colouring alone. Probably Leila would deny she had a daughter with her last breath.

Silently she edged up the staircase to the first landing, her bare feet making no sound. Halfway up she fancied she could smell coffee.

Of course she could smell coffee. The marvellous aroma was unmistakable. What sort of burglar would make himself coffee? It had to be some member of the family. A distant member, perhaps? One of the male cousins? That playboy, Greg? Just as she was hesitating, full of uncertainty, she heard footsteps in the long, spacious entrance hall with its marble tiling. Light, but simply not light enough to be a woman's. It was a male. Intruder or relation?

Her stomach contracted and her head went into a spin. Adrenalin pumped into her blood, otherwise she thought she wouldn't have been able to go a step further. As it was, she continued upwards. Someone was punching numbers into the security system. Why? They were already in. Or were they leaving? She felt a sharp ache at her temples, swayed a little, dropped the golf club.

You idiot!

If one accepted Murphy's Law, if anything could go wrong, it would. She did. The club landed with a clatter, the stick pinging off the shining brass balustrade of the wrought-iron staircase. A thousand miserable damns! She backed down a step or two, in a great hurry to retrieve the golf club. The noise of its falling would have alerted the intruder. Silence now roared at her.

Breathe in and out. Slow your pulse.

She readied herself. She didn't rate herself as fearless, but if something bad was about to overtake her she wouldn't let it pass without a fight.

Only, like a benediction came a voice. A deep, vibrant, sophisticated male voice. She would recognise it anywhere in the world. Probably even if she were out moon-walking.

"Miranda, is that you?"

Louder footsteps struck the marble tiles. She stood electrified. Panic thinly plastered over with stoicism gave way to an excitement so thrilling it was impossible to contain it.

It's me...it's me...it's me! She wanted to shout it from the rooftops.

Corin! Was that a birthday present or what?

"God, I thought I was being as quiet as the proverbial mouse," he called down to her.

"I'm here." She was practically whispering now, her mouth had gone so dry. Corin was *here*. She'd had only a forlorn hope he would even remember her birth date. But he was here! She didn't think she could climb the rest of the stairs, she was starting to shake so much. She had to take a moment to settle, to compose herself.

Corin!

This was the nearest she had ever come to euphoria. It was making her quite woozy.

"Where are you? On the stairs?" His footsteps were moving closer. "I'm sorry I woke you." His tone held both concern and apology. "I thought you'd be fast asleep."

Pull yourself together, silly. Think of your next move. No way can you act the gauche girl.

Only she couldn't seem to get her head around the fact Corin was here in the house. There had been no advance warning. Just his electrifying presence. Had Zara known, she would have told her. So that meant Zara didn't know either. She felt so unnerved, so totally off balance, she was almost ready to scuttle back down the stairs. She knew she looked perfectly presentable, with the kimono tied tightly around her, but the shock and wonder of his arrival was so enormously extravagant it was emotional agony.

All at once her knees gave way. She collapsed in a silken huddle on the step.

Corin appeared, taking in her small crumpled figure. "Oh, for God's sake, Miranda!" He hurried down to her, bringing with him the force field that always zoomed in on her. He was wearing evening dress. Black trousers, white pin-tucked shirt. The black bow tie was undone and left dangling. "I can't apologise enough!" He spoke very gently, getting an arm around her and lifting her to her feet. "I frightened you?"

"I have to say you did." From chills of fright, she was now bathed in the glorious heat of contact. It seared her lightly clad body that was pressed so alarmingly close to his. "Why didn't you let us know you were coming?" She ventured to lift her head, staring into his brilliant dark eyes.

"But that would have spoilt the surprise. Though I was taking a risk, wasn't I?" His expression went wry. "Surely that's one of my golf irons on the step?"

"I was hoping I wouldn't have to use it." She stayed within the curve of his arm and shoulder, for the moment physically unable to stand straight. The warmth and scent of him was the most powerful aphrodisiac.

"Oh, poor you!" he groaned. Still with his arm around her, he steered them up the rest of the stairs and from there along the corridor into the entrance hall. Once there, he dropped a kiss on the top of her silver-gilt curls. "A very happy birthday, Miranda. I can say that, as it's gone twelve."

"Thank you." The thrill of his presence was so *keen* it was like exquisite little pinpricks all over her skin. Plus there was the fear she would betray herself. "But you surely didn't fly into London to say that?" She managed to make it sound as though she was well aware he hadn't.

"Why not? You're twenty-one only once in your life." His dark eyes moved slowly, steadfastly over her. "You look well." Marvellously pretty would have said it better. Not a skerrick of make-up on her heart-shaped face, her mouth a delectable rose, and the lovely blue-green of the silk kimono matching her eyes, turning them to jewels. The silver-gilt curls still clung to her head, but he thought they were a little longer and expertly styled. Zara would know all the right places to take her. "I've made coffee. Would you like a cup, or do you want to go back to sleep?"

"Won't the coffee keep you awake?" She could only stand, staring at him. His white dress shirt was a wonderful foil for his deep tan.

"Who cares?" he said lightly, finding himself with a battle on his hands. He wanted to reach for her and draw her back into his arms. She fitted perfectly. At least take her hand. Frustrating, then, to have so many obstacles in the way. "I feel like one. Come along. You weren't really going to hit me with that golf club, were you?"

"I was going to ring the police."

"I'm so glad you didn't." He led the way into the large, beautifully designed kitchen. She and Zara had had many a meal here. Often she had done the cooking.

"You're so much better than I am!" Zara had declared.

True. Only unlike Zara she'd had years of helping prepare meals, in the end taking over the job completely for her mother, who had morphed into her grandmother.

God rest her loving soul.

"They wouldn't have been too happy, coming out this time of night—and for what?" Corin was saying, pulling her out of her thoughts. "It's all my fault. I take full responsibility. It's just that I remember you once told me you were out like a light as soon as your head hit the pillow."

"That's when I was studying hard," she admitted with a faint smile. "These days I'm doing little but enjoying myself. I've got used to the sounds of the house as well, and Zara is in Berlin."

"Yes, I know."

"So she *did* know you were coming?"

"No, she didn't." He glanced across at her, a delicate figurine wrapped in turquoise silk. She had no idea how alluring she was. Which was just as well. "I told you. It had to be a surprise. I knew about the Berlin meetings, however. She'll be back Tuesday anyway."

"Yes."

"So sit down."

This was one of those kitchens that didn't look like a kitchen. It looked more like an exceptionally inviting living area, big sparkling chandelier and all. The space was so large it could easily accommodate the marble-topped carved wood table, painted the same off-white as all the cabinetry and surrounded by six comfortable be-cushioned chairs.

She took one, conscious he was looking at her. She glanced up. Their eyes met. Married. Or was she imagining it?

"Hello!" he said, very gently.

Whatever it was, she could hardly speak for the force of her emotions. "And greetings to you." Even her voice shook, as though she had lost much of her habitual control. There was *something* in his tone; in the depths of his brilliant dark eyes.

Eyes say more than words ever can.

What were hers saying? That she wanted to leap up, go to him, hug him, tell him she had missed him *dreadfully*, for all the wonderful times she'd been having.

Common sense won over. This was Corin Rylance. Dalton Rylance's son and heir. A family worth billions. These were important people who mattered. Corin was way out of her league. For all she knew he could be about to tell her he was getting engaged when he went home. To the Atwood woman.

"What am I thinking of?" he asked himself with a quick frown. "Champagne is more in order than coffee. There's a bottle of Dom in the fridge. I think we might crack it. What do you say?"

"I guess it *should* be champagne," she agreed. She sounded so *polite*! No easy feat, when the level of excitement was rising at an alarming rate. She saw it as a flame that if only lightly fanned could turn into a dangerous blaze. Formality seemed as good as any defence mechanism.

Keep your deeper emotions out of it.

Sound advice.

"Twenty-one and don't you forget it," Corin said.

"So where have you been?" She inspected his tall elegant frame. "The evening clothes?" He looked so wonderful it made her feel strangely fretful, her legs restless.

"I spent the evening with old friends. I actually arrived in London from Rome late yesterday. Needed to catch up on my sleep. Had a business meeting this morning that lasted until lunch. I let Zara get away on her trip to Germany so I could move in."

She thought of something to distract her attention away from him. "Let me get the glasses." She rose swiftly on her small bare feet. "Zara and I often cat in here. In fact, we've had many an enjoyable late-night supper."

"She tells me you get on wonderfully well together." He lowered his handsome dark head to look into the well-stocked refrigerator.

"She's my honorary big sister."

He turned back, champagne bottle in hand, black eyes glittery. "Just don't make me your big brother."

She was surprised by his tone. "Why not?"

"I don't *feel* like your big brother."

His body language confirmed it. She felt a rush of emotion that was the equivalent to a huge jolt of adrenalin.

How can he possibly look at you like that if he doesn't like you?

Get real! Don't you mean he's attracted?

In the past few months, with all the socialising she had been doing, she had been made aware men found her very attractive. Viscount Walton, the famous ladies' man, for one. Now, for the first time, was there a tension and an *intimacy* between them? Maybe it was the lateness of the hour? The months of separation? All she knew was there was a star-bright, bursting sensation in her chest, as if sparkling, spinning, Catherine wheels were going off.

So what role does he want?

Don't invite disaster.

She tried to ignore her voices, reaching up to grasp two beautiful crystal flutes. They were kept on the shelf above other crystal wine glasses of varying sizes. Sheer nerves and a surfeit of emotion made her fingers uncharacteristically clumsy. To her utter embarrassment, the flute she had just barely grasped fell from her hand onto the tiled floor. The long stem remained intact, but the bowl shattered into glittering fragments that covered a surprisingly wide area.

"Oh, *no*! Sorry, sorry—I'm so sorry." She apologised over

and over. Emotion was her undoing. "How could I have been so clumsy?"

Corin moved in very quickly. "Stand right where you are," he instructed. "The glass has gone everywhere. Amazing how it can do that! You'd think the chandelier had fallen."

"I'll replace it."

Corin sounded totally indifferent to the damage. "Forget it, Miranda. It's only a glass."

"A very expensive glass." Her voice conveyed her distress and agitation.

"I said forget it," he responded rather tersely, as though her evident upset was getting to him. "Rather a broken glass than you cut your pretty feet. No slippers?"

"Extra quiet on the stairs," she explained shakily. "You could have been a burglar. Anyway, I'm fine. I'll get the broom." She unfroze, determined to sweep up the fragments, only Corin shocked her by reaching out for her and lifting her clean off her feet.

"I *said* stay put."

Her breathing had escalated to such a pitch it was darn nearly a whistle. "No need to turn cranky."

"I'm *not* cranky." He laughed.

"All the same, I was clumsy."

"You and clumsy don't go together."

It was precisely then that the silk sash of her kimono slid out of its knot and unfurled, making its sinuous way to the tiles, thus exposing Miranda's flimsy nightgown: fine white cotton caught by a deep V of crocheted lace that was threaded with blue satin ribbon. She had never felt so naked in her life.

"You *can't* hold me." Her nerves were coiled so tight they were about to snap.

"Does holding you change things, Miranda?" The amusement had gone out of his voice. It was oddly taut, as were the muscles in his lean, powerful body. Even his eyes were filled with a daunting yet exciting masculine intensity.

"I mean I must be h-heavy."

"You're a featherweight." He hoisted her higher, to prove his point, carrying her back to the table. "There—you can relax now!" He set her atop it, with a big blue pottery bowl filled with fat, juicy lemons just to her right. "Stay there. That's an order. I've opened the champagne. We're going to have a glass or two each. It's your birthday. I'm not going to allow anything to spoil it."

With his height, he reached easily into the top shelf, taking down two exquisite flutes while glass crunched beneath his gleaming black dress shoes. "Right! I'd better sweep this little lot up."

The odd tension between them resonated in the large room. She watched him sweep up the glass with a few swift, efficient movements, then push it into a pile, clearly sticking to his plan of pouring the champagne. That done, he handed her a frosted flute, his strong, elegant fingers closing momentarily around hers.

The pleasure was so sharp it was a wonder she didn't cry out.

"Congratulations, Miranda, on your twenty-first!" He toasted her. "May you have a long, happy, healthy and fulfilled life."

"And may I always know you and Zara," she returned emotionally. "The two of you have come to mean the world to this orphan."

"Listen to you!" he said gently. "Drink up. This is a great year."

She savoured the fine vintage wine, first in her mouth, experiencing the burst of delicious bubbles, then in the flavour, letting the wine run down her throat in a cold rivulet until the flute was empty. "Beautiful!" she breathed, her tongue retaining the cold, crisp after-taste.

"Then how come there's a little heartbreak in your voice?" he asked, finding her far more of an intoxicant than the most superb wine.

"I don't know, Corin. The significance of the moment?"

So many unsaid things were suddenly between them.

And then his hand came out. He touched the satin texture of her cheek.

She couldn't help it. She *moaned.* "I feel like I've known you all my life."

"So look at me."

She obeyed, looking directly into his brilliant eyes. Dark as they were, they couldn't hide the gleaming sensuality.

No distance at all now divided them. Both seemed possessed by the moment. "It's your birthday, so I believe I should be allowed to kiss you," he murmured, already dipping his head. "One kiss. That's all. On this very special occasion we might find it permissible to go out on a limb." He managed to speak lightly, affectionately, even, but in reality he was driven by pure desire that had to find at least some degree of release. Time to confront the repressed knowledge that his desire for her had begun the moment he had first laid eyes on her years before.

He wanted to run an urgent hand down the column of her throat to her delicate breasts. To his captive eyes they resembled pink-tipped white roses, not long out of bud. He wanted to feel her heartbeat beneath his palm. If only she were older, more experienced, more along the way with her ambitions, he would kiss her and caress her before carrying her to bed.

But this was Miranda. He couldn't allow his control to slip. He had vowed to look after her and her interests. She was *young*, when his experience of life and living had gone far beyond even his own age group.

From long practice Corin reined himself back to a pace he thought they both could handle. He set down his wine glass before taking hers out of her hand.

"Happy birthday, Miranda." His voice was low, and to Miranda's ears heart-stoppingly deep and romantic. Even before he touched her she felt as if she was being possessed. Gently he took her face between his hands, inhaling her sweet fragrance.

There can be no future in this.

Her warning voice tolled like a bell.

All you stand to gain is heartbreak.

At that moment she couldn't bring herself to care. She had to seize this one breathless instant. One kiss, then everything would go back to normal. They would return to their respective roles.

It doesn't work that way.

"Come here," he whispered.

All there was was a deep hunger. She moved her upper body into him, her spine curved, while he held her face and kissed her as if he had never in his life known a woman he wanted to kiss more. He kissed her not like Corin her mentor. He kissed her like the most ardent lover. It was a brilliant, beautiful, incredibly *real* kiss, as if for those short moments out of time he was declaring love for her. This was no quick flare of pleasure-seeking. None of the male's driving sex urge was on display. All control wasn't lost. The kiss was *contained*. A decision acted upon. But deeply, deeply erotic for all that.

One of you will get hurt. It won't be him. It will be you.

Corin found he had to pull his mouth away. Even with his exercising of strict control, the level of excitement had surged so high he thought it would take a long time to subside. "Has no one told you how beautiful you are, Miranda?" He gazed down on her face. It looked dreamy, almost somnolent, as though she had been transported to another place.

It took her long moments to answer. "If they have, I haven't taken much notice."

As an answer it was very revealing. Careful now, Corin thought. He would do nothing to threaten her well being. One kiss had proved more than enough to handle, luring him on while staying his hand. He moved his body back a little, deliberately lightening his tone. "Zara has mentioned many times how charming people find you. There's some old roué—what's his name? Walton?"

Her heart was racing so hard and fast it was moving the lace at her breast. "Eddie *is* quite a player." With an effort she summoned up a smile. She had taken their kiss in her stride, hadn't she? There was wisdom in caution. "There are many women in his life."

"But he wants to spend time with you?"

"Maybe he does. But I'm not anyone's passing fancy, Corin. I avoid danger and damage."

"Good." He turned away from temptation. "One more glass, then I must let you go back to bed. I need to turn in myself. We're off to Venice in the morning."

She was so startled she gave a little cry. "*What* did you say?"

Venice? Magic in the air.

She wished she was sitting in a chair, so she could ease back into it for support. As it was, she thought she might topple off the table.

"Venice. Probably the most fascinating city ever built by man," he said, busy refilling their sparkling flutes. "I have us booked into a first-class hotel. Tons of atmosphere. It's on the site of the orphanage church where Vivaldi probably dreamed up the Four Seasons. I think you'll love it. It's the quintessential Venetian luxury hotel and its position is superb. Our respective suites overlook the Lagoon, and it's only a few minutes' walk from the Piazza San Marco. It'll be a great experience for you. You're just the sort of young woman to fully appreciate it. The heart of a pure romantic beats beneath this Bachelor of Science."

She was perilously close to bursting into tears. "Corin, you don't have to do all this for me."

"What have I done for you really?" He held her with his compelling eyes.

"What no one else has done! You overwhelm me."

"What? Feisty little you?" he scoffed. "The teenager who launched herself into my lap? If that wasn't initiative, what is? Risky too, as you very well knew. Here—drink this down, then off to bed. A cab will be here at eight sharp to take us to the airport. Ninety minutes or so on we take off to Marco Polo International. We return to London Monday afternoon. I'll wait to see Zara when she comes back, then I'll be heading home for a few days before I head off to meet up with my father in China. Business, needless to say."

"This is like a fairy tale," Miranda breathed, accepting the crystal flute from him with visions of the legendary Serenissima she had seen only in books and films rising before her eyes.

"Well, your life hasn't exactly been a fairy tale up to date. This is by way of balance. Besides, even if we're not related by blood we do have a strong connection."

A shadow crossed her small heart-shaped face. "I want to tell Zara," she confessed. "We've become close. I don't like keeping my true identity from her."

"Only there might be quite a price to pay," he offered rather tensely. "For the moment anyway. I know how you feel. I don't keep secrets from my sister. I love her. After our mother was killed we were so *alone*, except for one another and our grandparents when we were allowed to see them. Dad did his best to isolate us, but he didn't succeed. A life of wealth and privilege doesn't guarantee happiness, that's for sure. The occasion *will* present itself. You just have to be patient."

"Until the timing fits in with *your* agenda, Corin?" There was just the tiniest hint of challenge in her tone.

"Trust me," he urged. "Right at the moment I'm most concerned with protecting you from what could be a very unpleasant experience."

"You feel contempt for Leila, don't you?" she said, sadly aware this woman was her mother.

He gave a nonchalant shrug, but the expression on his handsome face had darkened. "Leila is a very destructive woman. My father can't see it, but Leila's whole being is centred on *self*. Valiant as you are, clever as you are, you'd be no match for her. You see life very differently from your mother, Miranda. You want to *serve*. Leila only wants to *take*."

"Does she want to take *you*?" The instant it was out of her mouth she felt a great spasm of shock. *Why* had she broached such a highly dangerous and emotive subject? Could it have been acute feminine intuition at work? There *was* such a thing. Corin's father was still a very handsome man. But Corin was young. He was much closer in age to Leila than his father. And Corin was *blindingly* sexy.

"Only *you* could get away with saying that." He turned her face to him, fingers closing around her pointed chin.

"So forgive me." She was actually appalled at herself. "But you make her sound such a rapacious woman."

His hand dropped. "She makes my father happy. Zara and

I might wish she had never come into our lives, but she did. My father is a business giant, a brilliantly clever man, but in some respects he's completely under Leila's domination."

"And this is the woman who bore me?" she said, a dismal note in her voice.

"You are *you*," he replied with strong emphasis. "All your admirable characteristics come from a different source."

"Oh, I hope so," she gasped. "My grandparents were fine people. They formed me. But then they would have done their best to form Leila. Perhaps my father, whoever he may be, made some sort of a contribution?" she suggested with some irony. "There are many mysteries in life, aren't there? A lot of them I would think unsolved."

His expression had turned brooding. "I agree. It's possible that whoever your father was he didn't know Leila was pregnant."

"So where did she get the money to run away? My grandparents didn't have anything. She didn't rob a bank. Someone gave it to her."

"Someone who might have been appalled by the whole situation. It could be a real grief, Miranda. Anyway, we won't talk about it any more. It's your birthday."

"Do you think Leila will remember?" she asked with a twist of bitterness.

"If she does she won't flail herself." His answer was full of contempt. "Promise me you'll put Leila out of your mind. I'm planning a long festive weekend. Promise?"

She threw up her shining head. "I promise," she said.

"Then drink up and we'll go to bed."

If only! If only! If only!

CHAPTER THREE

THERE followed the most glorious day of her life. The word *dazzling* should be kept for the rarest occasions, Miranda thought. A private mini-bus was waiting at Marco Polo airport to take them to their water taxi, which again had to be private, because they had it all to themselves. What it is to be rich! Miranda mused, all but mesmerised by this whirl of luxury and dream trips to fabled locations. With her particular mind set, another thought inevitably struck her. One would need to be sprightly when visiting Venice, with all the getting in and out of water craft. She had to think of the elderly, and people with back and knee problems. Mercifully, at the grand old age of twenty-one, her body was wonderfully flexible.

In a haze of unbounded pleasure and excitement she moved ahead of Corin into the cabin, and from there into the sunshine at the rear of the *vaporetto*. There was so much to take in. So much to capture the imagination. The triumph of Venice, a city built on water! At times like this she would have given almost anything to be an artist. She could scarcely believe she, Miranda Thornton, raised by ordinary country folk, the people who had loved her the most, yet who had kept secret from her the fact she had been abandoned by her mother as an infant, was now entering upon the most glorious street in the world.

A street that had been immortalised by some of history's truly great artists. Canaletto immediately sprang to mind. And the great English painter J. M. W. Turner. She had adored Turner's work on her gallery trips with Zara, who was very knowledgeable about art. Turner had really spoken to her. Then there was the American John Singer Sargent, who had painted many scenes of Venice. And why not?

The sheer grandeur was breathtaking: the splendid frontages of the magnificent palaces—Venetian Byzantine, Gothic, Renaissance—that lined either bank of the famous waterway with a hot sun beating down. She felt as though she was absorbing the palpable sense of history—of a city founded in the fifth century—through her pores, though it was near impossible to absorb the totality of the scene, so much splendour was on show.

The water was an indescribable blue-green. Not sparkling, like the waters of home, but with a kind of lustre like oil spreading out over the surface of the great canal, thus picking up marvellous reflections. She wondered what Venice would look like at night. And she was *here*! It made one have faith in miracles.

"Well?" asked Corin, studying her enchantingly pretty face. From the moment he had met her he had found her fascinating—not just her highly distinctive looks, but her manner, her speech, the sense of purpose that even at seventeen had emanated from her. He and Zara had visited Venice, a favourite city of their mother's, many times before, but this time with Miranda, brand-new to the fabled Serenissima, he found his own pleasure expanding by the minute.

She turned to him eagerly with a spontaneous smile, turquoise eyes glittering. "It's beyond—way beyond—my expectations. The extraordinary light!"

"The golden glow of Venice," he said.

"The colour of the water is indescribable!"

"From a height it shimmers," he told her. "Anyone familiar with our waters in Australia speaks about the dazzling blue sparkle, but the Grand Canal—indeed all the waters of Europe—have a different palette and a different character." He studied her flawless white skin with the luminosity of alabaster. "Are you wearing sun block?"

She shook her head almost guiltily. "No." She had meant to put some on. Not that she had needed it so far in London.

He tut-tutted. "And you a doctor in the making. It's very hot, and it will get hotter as the day wears on. It's a different heat from ours, as I'm sure you've already noticed. Come back inside. Don't worry. We'll see everything. Take a gondola ride. The gondolas can reach the narrowest and most shallow canals. It's the best way to get around. These days it costs an arm and a leg, but you learn the city from both sides of the canal. There's a tremendous amount to see, but we have to make the best choices to fit in with our time. We might manage a visit to the island of Murano."

"World-renowned for its glass-making. I do know that." She had a girlfriend whose parents had brought her back a beautiful necklace and earrings set from Murano.

He nodded. "For centuries they were the only craftsmen in the whole of Europe who knew the secret of making mirrors. They held on to the technique for all that time."

"I'm not surprised." She laughed. "It would have brought in a great deal of money as well as prestige."

"Exactly. There's a very fine museum on the island called Palazzo Guistinian. Thousands of pieces cover the entire history of glassmaking from the ancient Egyptians to the present day."

"Wasn't there some Bond movie when they sent a cabinet toppling?" She frowned, trying to remember. Was it an older movie, with a marvellously handsome Roger Moore?

"Wouldn't be a bit surprised," he said wryly. "They sent a *palazzo* toppling into the Grand Canal for the first one featuring the new James Bond, Daniel Craig. If you like I can arrange a water taxi so we can go over on our own. Only a short trip."

"That would be wonderful, Corin. But I must admit I'm a bit worried about how much money you must be spending." A fortune already, in her reckoning.

"Don't feel guilty. I've got it. One of the perks of being a Rylance."

She watched him closely. He had only been standing in the sun a short time, but she could have sworn his golden tan had deepened. "It's sad and strange, isn't it, that you and Zara, brought up with such wealth, haven't had a happy life?"

"And you all of twenty-one!" He gave her a smile.

"Okay, okay!" She drew in a quick breath. "But please let me tell you I'll never forget this birthday if I live another eighty years." It came out with enormous gratitude and a tiny quiver of sob.

Instantly, he enfolded her in a brief hug, as if she was his favourite cousin. "So why do you think I brought you?" he said.

Her suite overlooked a great breadth of the luminous waterscape, looking towards the island of San Giorgio. She could see its magnificent church, San Giorgio Maggiore with its Renaissance façade, gleaming white in the sun, and the imposing *campanile*—the bell tower. The bedroom's décor was like no other she had ever seen. Sumptuous, seductive, otherworldly in its way, with antique furniture, fine art, fragrances on the air—and she thought a delicious touch of spookiness. But then she did have a great deal of imagination.

As she stood there, marvelling, Corin turned to face her for a moment, with amused and indulgent dark eyes. "I don't like to drag you away, but I must. A quick lunch, then as much as we can comfortably fit in of a grand tour, before dinner here. The hotel has a very fine restaurant and chef. Then we take in the city by night. Don't forget the sun block."

"I wish I could say in Italian your wish is my command."

"Then let me say it for you."

She applauded as he broke into fluent Italian. "*Non parlo Italiano,* I'm afraid," she smiled. "Apart from the usual one liners. *Arriverderci, addio, ciao,* and the like—and what I've picked up from Donna Leon's Venice-based books. I really enjoy her charming *Commissario Brunetti.* I studied Japanese at school, but I had to concentrate on Maths, Physics and Chemistry. Not much time available for languages, I'm sorry to say."

"You've got plenty of time to learn," he said casually. "This won't be your last trip to Italy, Miranda. This is your *first.*"

She couldn't help it. She clapped her hands. "Prophecies already? Marvellous!"

"Don't mention it," he said.

She knew she would be having flashbacks of this fabulous trip to Venice for the rest of her life. In a single afternoon and evening they had packed in as much as they possibly could see of what had to be the most fascinating and mysterious city on earth. The fact that Corin spoke fluent Italian and knew the city so well proved to be an enormous advantage. She was free to soak up so many dazzling sights and scenes, buildings and churches. The famous Basilica of San Marco the focal point of the great *piazza*, Santa Maria della Salute. She loved the art, the sculpture—it was like partaking of a glorious banquet. Corin kept up a running commentary. She listened. They took a gondola ride. When they walked it was hand in hand. She knew he was keeping her close to his side, but they might have been lovers. Except they weren't. Nor could they be. Theirs was no conventional friendship, yet Miranda had never felt more close to anyone in her life.

When they met up for dinner he greeted her with a low, admiring, "*Come sei bella*, Miranda!"

Although he had adopted the lightest of tones, something in his expression made her throat tighten and tears prick at the back of her eyes. *Did* he find her beautiful? She had tried her hardest to be. For him. She had packed a short glittery silver dress, little more than a slip, but she was slim and petite and it did touch in all the right places and show off her legs. She well remembered the lovely day shopping with Zara, who had picked the gauzy dress out for her.

"It's you exactly, Miri!"

Pleasures! Ecstasies! She had allowed them to enter her life. Now she began to fear their power. She realised with a degree of shock that she didn't know herself very well. She had thought herself as a calm, contained person, well in control. A young woman with a brain perfectly designed for study: taking in reams of information and retaining it. She had a serious purpose in life. What she had to confront now was the fact that beneath the containment, her serious ambitions in life, she had a very passionate nature. And it was Corin who had unlocked it.

Dinner was absolutely brilliant; the *sala da pranzo* richly appointed. Wherever her eyes rested it was on something beautiful. The hotel was renowned for its collection of artwork, all on display for the pleasure of their guests. They had a table for two looking directly across the lagoon at San Giorgio Maggiori. To her delight it was all lit up for the night.

Dishes materialised as if by magic. A superb mingling of flavours, combinations and textures; the finest, fresh ingredients; the presentation a work of art. In the background soft harmonious chamber music added to the ambience. Vivaldi, most likely. His famous church the Pieta was just next door. Her choice of dessert was a bitter chocolate mousse with coffee granita and ginger cream. It simply melted in her mouth. Corin's choice was a classic *tiramisu* she thought had to be carried to the highest level of perfection.

"This has been so groaningly delicious I think we'll take a stroll before bed," he suggested. They had finished coffee, and now he motioned to their discreetly attentive *cameriere*.

"Yes, of course. Good idea!"

She didn't want the night to end. But Corin had arranged a tour of the Grand Canal in a private *vaporetto* in the morning, including a trip to the Guggenheim, the great heiress Peggy Guggenheim's former home, right on the Grand Canal, now one of Europe's premier museums devoted to modern art. This might have been Miranda's gap year, but no gap was being left unfilled. She was having a wonderful time. Small wonder the children of the wealthy were granted their finishing year in Europe. It added a fine polish. And there was nothing in the world like first-hand experience.

Outside the door of her suite, Corin tucked a breeze-ruffled curl behind her ear. "Sleep well. Lots to do tomorrow."

They had returned from their stroll around the great *piazza*, along with the summer tourists enjoying the warmth and beauty of their surroundings, her arm tucked cozily in his. Now it was time to say goodnight.

"I can't thank you enough for this trip, Corin." She looked up to meet those brilliant, intense eyes. He had such an aura. She could only imagine it would increase with the years. "You and Zara have been wonderful to me."

"You don't think it's because you're easy to be wonderful to?" he asked with a smile. "You're so receptive to new experiences, Miranda. You undoubtedly have an eye. I know you've added a considerable lustre to *my* stay. Now, goodnight. Breakfast at eight. Okay?"

"Fine. My first night in a huge canopied Venetian bed. This is such an alluring place!" She threw up her arms.

Did she know just how alluring *she* was? Corin thought as he moved resolutely away. All those fascinating changes of expression! Every minute he spent with her bound him closer and closer. It had taken all his resolve to walk away, pretending light affection, when he hungered to pick her up, take her to her Venetian bed and make endless love to her. She was twenty-one. Was she still a virgin? Had the usual experimentation gone on? Not with her Peter. He was sure of that. But with another intelligent, caring young man? Miranda wouldn't settle for less. She was now very much a part of his life. He had no intention of letting her get away. But it would take time. Such was his high regard for her and her ambitions he was prepared to wait.

Only he was human, and he wanted her so much it was *pain*.

The bathroom of her suite was magnificent, lavishly covered in Italian marble. The finest bath and body products were to hand, and robe and slippers. Miranda took a quick shower and emerged glowing. She dried herself off, slipped on her nightdress and her own satin robe, then padded into the bedroom with the panoramic tiny terrace beyond. Truth be told, she felt too keyed-up to sleep. She had thought the warm shower followed by a quick cool blast would quell all the stirrings in her body. But just the opposite. This intense awareness of herself as a woman, the awareness of her body, had been brought about by Corin. His brilliant dark eyes as he had said goodnight had been hooded—just the broad, high sweep of his cheekbones. Was that to hide his thoughts? They had connected on many levels, but the physical one was definitely there. She had *seen* it. She had *felt* it when he took her face between his hands. So much was transmitted by touch. Whatever he felt, however, he wasn't going to do a thing about it. In his position he would be weighing up the consequences. She wasn't the only one with defence strategies. Did he consider a sexual relationship with her taboo? Technically she was his stepsister, wasn't she? Was there a liability attached to having a physical relationship?

Feeling a wave of sweet melancholy, she picked up her crystal-backed brush to give her hair its ritual thirty strokes. Forget one hundred. Mentally she had long dreamed of Corin as her lover. Incredibly stupid of anyone to hanker for someone out of their reach. Her past lovers had been infrequent. Two, actually. Both fellow students, both in love with her, both very tender in their ministrations. She had wanted to know what making love was all about. She hadn't found much of an answer in either short-lived experience. She had considered at those times she mightn't be capable of giving herself completely to anyone. Look what had happened to her mother. She didn't understand her mother's life. It was crucial she understood her own.

That was when she casually looked up, glancing into the ornately carved pier mirror in front of her.

A man was staring back at her, his body as solid and impenetrable as a stone statue.

The level of shock was bottomless. She drew in a sharp breath that quivered like an arrow in flight. A judder racked her spine. Yet not a single word burst from her throat. No scream. No cry at all.

Somehow she kept upright, determined to stay that way. He was dressed very *oddly*. He might have stepped out of another century. Could it be some sort of fancy dress? Venice was famous for it. But even as she considered that she had to reject it.

Push back the panic.

He remained eerily still. Where had he sprung from? The terrace? Had he been hiding out there? Had he slipped in earlier in the night when the maid came in to turn down the bed?

"What are you *doing* here?" she cried as she spun to confront him. Aggression seemed the best way to go, though some part of her brain had signalled he meant her harm.

She required an explanation.

Only she was by herself.

Quite, quite *alone*.

How could that be? A kind of dread started cold in her veins. She had a well-organised mind. She was certain she wasn't losing it. Her eyes darted all around the room. This was alarming. He'd had no time to get anywhere within a framework of seconds. There had to be a logical explanation. Yet her view of life as she had known it started to waver. The parameters were suddenly blurred. She leaned against the canopied bed. Had he stepped out of a parallel universe? Was there any such thing? Many people believed there was, but she was far too rational to believe in—

Ghosts?

The word presented itself, only it was seriously weird. She'd had more than a glimpse of her visitor. It couldn't have been a trick of the light. More than a touch of dizziness beset her. The air had definitely chilled around her. Indeed, the opulent room was filled with an impenetrable thick silence, as if she had cotton wool stuffed into her ears. Except she could distinctly hear the tinkling of the chandelier above her head. Something had set the lovely crystal lustres in motion.

There was no breeze.

Sometimes life can depart from the easily explained.

It had to be a trick of the light. Her imagination. The legendary mystique of Venice at work?

She made a big effort to get control of herself. None of those explanations would wash. What she saw, she *saw*. No way was she crazy or mildly intoxicated. The walk after dinner had cleared her head in any case. Already a strong suspicion was with her. There just could be a paper-thin wall between this world and *that*. The majority of the population managed to keep it at arm's length. But many learned people, academics and the like—one had to discount the fanciful—had theorised that ghosts *did* exist. And they were notorious for hanging around castles and palaces.

She was fairly sure now what her visitor was.

An apparition.

One she had done nothing to summon up. Her mind's eye retained a snapshot of that long, narrow face, the black beard, the shoulder-length dark hair, the strange dress like a priest's cassock. His hands, as white as his face, had been quietly folded. A glinting medallion hung around his neck. He hadn't appeared hazy. Quite the contrary. He'd been substantial. Someone strong enough to materialise if only for a moment.

Energy, perhaps? Something of a person that lingered in the atmosphere? She was striving to rationalise what she had seen.

Only she was certain she wouldn't be able to sleep here. Imagine if he came back again? Imagine if he sat down on the side of the bed?

If anyone had asked her that morning if she believed in ghosts she would have laughed and quoted some lines from *Hamlet*:

> "There are more things in Heaven and Earth, Horatio,
> Than are dreamt of in your philosophy."

She wasn't laughing now. She was a quaking bundle of nerves.

Corin answered the phone almost immediately. *"Pronto!"*

"It's me," she said at a rush, ashamed of the tremor in her voice. "Can you please come down to my suite? *Now!*"

His answer was sharp. "You're okay? What's happened?"

"I'll tell you when you arrive."

She needed his strong arms to enclose her. His powerful presence. At least whatever she had seen was long gone. How did ghosts come by their clothes anyway? she pondered weakly. Did they have access to communal wardrobes? She began to feel mildly hysterical. Jewellery pools? How did he manage to hold onto the medallion he wore around his neck?

What she had so briefly experienced had opened up a nest of snakes. She didn't feel at all foolish. She had her wits about her. She had seen what she had seen for long enough to be sure.

Vast relief swept her as Corin strode in. His thick, lustrous hair was tousled into deep waves. He wore a white T-shirt and jeans, hurriedly pulled on.

"For God's sake, Miranda, you're as white as a sheet. What's happened? Did something frighten you?" He looked at her, then beyond her, obviously searching the room, and then just as she had hoped he reached for her and drew her into his arms, clamping her close. "It's okay. I'm here." Solid warm flesh, strong arms, vibrantly male. She could feel the strength and power in him. The dizziness eased.

"And am I glad!" she muttered into his warm chest. "Listen, I don't want to make an issue of it—wake up the manager, demand an exorcism—but I think I've had a visit from Signor Vivaldi." She was capable now of attempting a joke.

He drew back a little so he could stare into her eyes. "What are you talking about? Did someone get in here?"

She shook her head. "Trust me. It was Signor Vivaldi. Only he wasn't carrying his violin. Don't let go!" she cried out as his grip slackened in his surprise.

"I won't." He sounded gentle, but perplexed. "Come and sit down." He led her, still with his arms around her, to the sofa, upholstered in rich scarlet, amber and gold brocade to match the bedspread and the hangings around the canopied bed.

"Do *you* believe in ghosts, Corin?" she asked, staring into his eyes. "Serious question, here. And please don't laugh."

"Who's laughing?" he answered soberly. Indeed, there was no trace of a laugh in his face or his voice. "Are you telling me you saw a ghost?"

"Right there in the mirror," she said. "Go on. Take a look. You're so tall and strong you'll probably frighten him off."

"More like he'd frighten *me*!" Corin rose to his feet, moving position so he could stare into the ornate antique pier glass.

"I confess I'm only getting a reflection of you," he said. She looked profoundly shaken, but it was obvious to him she was trying hard to keep herself together. That impressed him.

"The brain does funny things sometimes. Miranda," he said very gently. "Both Zara and I saw our mother in all sorts of places for ages after she'd gone. On the landing. The stairs. The end of the hallway. The rose gardens especially. It's grief. It's trying to come to terms with it. The sense of loss drives you to conjure up the loved one's presence."

Her eyes filled with tears. "Of course, Corin. I understand about you and Zara. I've had my own moments with my grandparents, but I knew them for what they were. I don't know this guy. I'm pretty clear-headed. Strong-minded, if I say so myself. I wasn't hallucinating. I'm not losing my marbles. I know what I know. I saw what I saw."

Corin resisted any attempt to convince her she had to be mistaken. "Well, it wasn't Vivaldi. He had *red* hair. He was called the Red Monk."

"Then it was one of his cronies. The whole place is intrinsically spooky. It wasn't my imagination. The whole experience was beyond eerie. He didn't look particularly dangerous, but I don't fancy seeing him again."

"I bet you don't !" Corin agreed on the instant. The weird thing was he believed her. Or believed her enough not to contradict her. "We'll swap suites."

Miranda reacted fast. "How do I know he won't follow me to yours?"

"I wouldn't blame him if he did." His answer was wry.

"This isn't a joke, Corin," she told him sharply. "You have to stay with me."

"What? Share the bed?" He had to try to inject some humour into a situation that was threatening to get out of hand.

"*You* can have the bed," she said magnanimously. "I'll sleep on this sofa. It's big and it's very comfortable. We might shift it closer to the bed, though."

"So we can hold hands?"

"Do you believe me or not?" she challenged. "Or do you think this is some kind of idiotic ploy to entice you here?"

"Never occurred to me." He kept his voice serious.

"If he'd been real I would have attacked him with my hair-brush. But there was no one. I suppose the fascination of Venice, apart from its beauty, mystery and exoticism, is that it's tantalisingly spooky. Part of the mythology, isn't it?"

He fetched up a sigh. "So my mother always said. As for me, I keep an open mind about ghosts. I have to admit it would take a lot to convince me. I do believe, however, *you* are convinced. Now, I have a suggestion. Why don't I take you down to my suite? Let you see what you think?"

"No way!" She rejected the offer. "You have to stay here with me. The air changed, you know. It was like I had wads of cotton wool stuffed in my ears, except I could hear the tinkling of the chandelier."

"It isn't tinkling now," he said somewhat dryly.

"Of course it isn't!" She struck his arm. "He's *gone*. Buzzed off. Maybe he has a full roster tonight? Some people are into the paranormal big-time. The thing is he looked just like he would have looked in life. Not some ectoplasm I could walk through. Stay with me, Corin. This is the most beautiful place in the world, but it *is* scary."

He released a long groan, feeling the onset of a raging torrent of emotions. "How can I possibly sleep in the bed and leave you on the sofa?"

"The bed's big enough for both of us," she said, trying to persuade him with the appeal in her turquoise eyes.

He groaned louder. "Miranda, there's not a bed in the world big enough for both of us. What do you think's going on here? You're a beautiful girl, and I'm as frail as the next guy."

"No, you're not," she said. "Not once you make up your mind. And you *have* made it up, haven't you?"

He gave a soundless laugh. "How do you know my best intentions won't fall into ruins?"

"If they do, it's *our* secret," she said. "We have secrets, don't we, Corin?"

"Boy, are you full of surprises!" he exclaimed. "You're saying you'll sleep with me?"

"I'm desperate."

He laughed aloud. "Miranda, I can't sleep on the sofa. I'm too big. You can. We can't share the bed. You know as well as I do that's pushing it too far. My job is to look after you."

"Well, I didn't say you have this terrible aching longing for me, did I? You're not by any chance getting engaged when you go home?"

"Miranda, engagements are the last thing on my mind." The expression on his handsome face turned severe.

"Me too. So take it easy. Can you sleep in your jeans?"

"You bet I can."

"Thank you for coming, Corin," she said. "I'm not making this up. I'm sure of what I saw."

"Then you're a very lucky girl!" he offered darkly. "You'll be dining off the experience for years." He rose to his six foot plus, giving vent to a disturbed sigh. "Okay, I take the bed."

"I'll just curl up here on the sofa," she said, immensely grateful for his presence. The force in him overrode all sense of trepidation. The worst of the trembling had stopped. "You can throw me the silk throw, if you would."

"Anything, my lady." He picked it up and passed it to her.

"Can we keep a light on in the sitting room?" she asked, settling herself with the luxurious silk throw over her.

"I don't see why not." He moved into the other room,

switching on a single lamp, with its golden pool of illumination. "I just knew in my bones this was going to be a memorable stay. Shut your eyes and go to sleep now, Miranda. Your ghost will know better than to return."

CHAPTER FOUR

SOMETHING drew him out of a tormented sleep. His body was still vibrating, unable to shut down. It had taken him ages to settle into a doze, but at least Miranda had lapsed into sleep almost immediately. Shock, of course. She was a highly intelligent, level-headed young woman. He had to believe she had seen *something*. Whatever it was, it wasn't about to bother him. Or he sure as hell wasn't worried. What worried him was that sex was very much on his mind. Sex with Miranda. God knew it was normal enough to want to make love to a young woman who held him in thrall. But not now—not like this. It seemed to him too much like taking advantage. That he could not do. But try telling that to his powerfully aroused body.

Decency must override desire, Corin.

He was getting a bit tired of his conscience blasting him.

Only the unthinkable had happened. Miranda had crept into bed beside him and now rolled lightly against his back, her petite body with its soft curves and light bones nestled up against his flesh. Tension tore through him. His heart set up a loud tattoo, beating in his ears with the volume turned full on. He turned very carefully, fighting not to give a strangled moan. He was lying beneath the coverlet. She was lying on top of it.

My God, what do I do next?

His whole body was throbbing, stirred into flaming life. He could barely stay in his skin. Desire was a burning fever. He would have coped with half a dozen Venetian ghosts far better than this intensely desirable young woman curled up against him. The lightness of her! The fragrance! A man could drown in it. The only course open to him was to retreat, slide out of the other side of the bed. He could prop himself up on the sofa for the rest of the night. Get comfortable somehow. See it out until morning. Ghosts didn't hang around in the light of day. They were too tired out from their nocturnal excursions. Or was that vampires? Either way, he didn't care. Miranda was the real problem.

"Corin?" Just to make the problem near unsolvable, she suddenly sat up, twisting her shining head towards him. Her voice was hushed, but filled with urgency. "Don't go away. Please don't. I didn't like the sofa much. I wanted to be closer."

"Miranda, stop it," he begged.

You're losing it, Corin!

"I can't stay here in this bed with you," he said tautly. "You're nobody's fool. My whole body is hurting. I'll make love to you. Nothing surer!"

"Then do it!" she burst out, sounding as though she knew far better than he did. "Ease the pain. This is *life*! I've decided I want to live it. None of us knows how much time we have, do we? Why waste what we've got? You're alive. I'm alive. If you like, when we wake up we can pretend it was all a dream."

"And you think there's going to be a lot of comfort in that?" he demanded, aghast. He reached for her, took hold of a bare delicate shoulder where her robe had fallen off. He could see the silver shimmer of her hair, like radiant moonlight. "Are you or are you not a virgin?"

"Will that improve or detract from my status?" she challenged. "Technically I'm not, but I *can* say in all truth the earth has never moved for me. I've had two lovers. Really nice guys. Fellow students. Smart, good-looking. Not untried either. But I couldn't for the life of me see what all the fuss was about. Perhaps you can tell me? I'm sure you've had plenty of experience."

"And you'd like me to share it with you?" he asked acidly. "Does this give me the go-ahead?"

A golden glow was spilling out of the sitting room. She could easily make out the hard tension in his face. "Oh, God, that's up to you!" she moaned, embarrassment welling, but not enough to drown the yearning. "I've had more thrills from your touching my cheek than ever I got from my previous experiences. You can multiply that by one thousand. Such are your erotic skills. Once I thought I couldn't give myself to anyone. Not after my mother. Not after her falling pregnant as a schoolgirl. Abandoning me. It altered my life. Maybe altered me in a radical way. Do you understand?"

"No, I damned well do not." He was merciless. He had to be.

"You're weighing up the consequences?" she asked.

"Miranda, this is madness," he groaned. But then, hadn't it been madness from the moment she had literally catapulted into his life?

"There are always consequences, I suppose. One or both of us could be hurt. But you're not married. I'm not married. Neither of us is in any great rush."

He gave a harsh laugh. "Either you go back to the sofa or I do."

"No, stay. *Please.* I'm not asking you to love me. I'm asking you to *make* love to me. There's a big difference. You said you wanted to, so just *do* it."

"And perhaps make you pay for it?" He showed the full

heat of his anger and arousal. "I don't walk around with condoms in my pocket. Oh, my God, Miranda, what are we talking about?" he asked in an agonised voice. Never in his life had he faced such temptation.

"Making love. You may not care to hear it, but I'm on the pill. I believe in being prepared. I'm not saying with you. I never dreamt we'd be here together like this. But I could have met someone. You never know. I'm a modern girl. This is right. For tonight, Corin. I know it in my soul. I didn't set out to seduce you. You had no intention of seducing me, such are your stringent scruples and code of morality. The ghost actually did us a favour."

"Oh, be quiet! Truly, *be quiet!*" He pulled her across him, wrapping his arms around her. She had to know what she was doing to him, but she didn't seem to care. "This is madness!"

"But splendid madness!" She let her head fall against his chest. She would remember this extraordinary night in the last dying seconds of her life.

"To put yourself in my hands?" His vibrant voice turned steely.

"Yes, yes, and *yes*! Put it down to shock. Shock has made me shameless. *'My heart, by many snares beguiled, Has grown timorous and wild!'* Some poet said that. Can't think who."

She allowed her body to spread out over his: fantastic feeling, utter abandon. Then she locked her bare, slender arms around his neck. She wasn't herself at all. She was a Miranda she had never known. Had her otherworldly visitor put a sensual spell on her? Maybe that was what he'd come for?

The agony of it! Corin felt every muscle shift in his lean body. His head was nearly bursting with conflicting emotions. Should he? Shouldn't he? The truth was he was already lost. He let his crow-black head fall back against the piled-up pillows like a man defeated. Such extreme sexual agony demanded release. There could be no ease without action. He wanted her. God, how he wanted her! Yet for a split second he faltered. Was it possible this perfect creature with her beautiful turquoise eyes was after *revenge*? Did she count this the right time? Had she *really* seen anything? Or was she winding him up? It could all be an elaborate scam. Some kind of weird payback? She was extremely intelligent. Highly rational. Very possibly an accomplished actress. Was she indeed playing him for a fool? If so, it was working!

Momentarily maddened, he turned her onto her side. That too was dangerously erotic, increasing the sexual tension. Then he put a hand to her tender neck, his fingers on that pulsing vein. Her flesh was like lustrous satin, as warm and as flushed as a rose. He wasn't *her* captor, though. That was the trouble, he thought with a tiny stab of hostility. She had captured *him*. Delilah bringing another Samson to his knees.

"Look at me. Kiss me," she whispered. "Before I dissolve right away."

Her little sigh was quite audible in the deeply shadowed room. He answered darkly. "What man can resist such witchcraft? Okay, Miranda, if this is what you want."

With one wrench, he had the coverlet on the floor, and then he pulled her to him, never more excruciatingly aware that passion was heedless of anything but itself. Such was his appetite, his mouth crushed hers…covered its sweetness completely…his tongue making triumphant entry into the moist apple-fresh interior. The kiss was punishing at first, ruthless, explosive, raw in its conquest. As he'd intended it to be. A futile show of male superiority? Only very quickly the fierceness gentled into something miraculous…utterly voluptuous…undreamed of rapture!

She was working her magic, turning the key to a heart he had thought locked safely away.

He paused for a moment, holding her hips, his head bent above her. He could see that her jewelled eyes were tightly shut. Her limbs were wound around his like tendrils, curved and curled. She was beautiful to him. Beautiful beyond belief. He could no more have stopped kissing her, no more stopped his hands from moving to shape and caress her small perfect breasts, than he could have stopped his own breath.

She was right. This was living. This was *life*!

They were entering into it together. No matter the consequences.

The moments of astonishing sensuality spun on and on, until he could no longer tolerate a shred of clothing to separate skin from skin. He had to unwrap her from her robe—it had almost fallen off her—then her nightgown, flinging both garments away. He looked back for the switch on the lamp. She seemed to shake her head, but he took no notice.

"Don't refuse me." He turned back to her, fully exposed to his sight; she was beautifully, delicately nude, like some lovely painting, showing lustrous skin tones. In one sweeping movement he slid his hand in a widening circle around her taut but pliant stomach, stopping to within an inch of the sensitive delta between her legs. "I want to *see* you. I want to kiss every inch of you. I want you to know you're exquisite to my eyes. And you *wanted* this, Miranda, remember."

Wanted it? She was half mad with longing. Pelted with it. She made a soft, helpless sound that was like a wail. He cut it off with his mouth.

Every cell in Miranda's body was a live wire of sensation. It was impossible not to respond to such mastery. She might never have been kissed or touched in her life before now.

He placed her exactly as he wanted her. Then he began to play her like a superbly crafted instrument. Perfect for a man's hand, its pitch exact, and capable of displaying a glorious range of emotions. He had never had a woman respond to his lovemaking with such passion and urgency. He had never felt within himself so wild an elation. He found he was shaping words, *saying* words—what were they? She had him totally in her power. Did it matter? All he knew was this was ecstasy, as fabulous as it was strange to him.

She could be your downfall.

He was more than willing to risk it. He needed to throw off his own clothes. Naked, he returned to the bed, where she pulled him down to her, glittery tears standing in her eyes.

"No—oh, *no*, Miranda, don't cry." Her tears stayed him. He leaned over her, supported by his strong arms, overtaken by a powerful sense of protectiveness.

"I'm *not* crying," she protested, reaching up to sink her fingers into his thick hair, all tousled waves and curls, tugging at it in her passion. "I'm on fire!"

Any glimmer of uncertainty vanished into thin air. Air that seemed scented by hundreds of glowing, unimaginably beautiful flowers. None of this had been premeditated, he thought, yet he had the absolute certainty both of them were in their rightful place. Slowly, voluptuously, on a surge of exultation, he covered her smooth-as-silk body with his own, still controlling his far more substantial weight with his arms while she clutched his naked back, her voice an emotional little sob.

"Love me!"

"For hours. Hours and hours on end." He was confronted with a searing truth. He wasn't just in love with Miranda. He wanted her with him for as long as he lived.

That in itself presented intractable problems.

But not tonight.

Tonight a miracle had been offered.

Miracles demanded they be grasped with both hands.

For the rest of their stay problems became irrelevant. Time out of mind. They both knew it. For those few precious days they lived their lives in a glorious conflict-free zone. Conflict would come later. There could be no avoiding it. There was always Leila. Leila had to be regarded as a most serious threat. She could potentially end the emotional journey they had embarked upon. But for now even the ghost was invited to come back if he so wished. He declined. No doubt he had a full book of hauntings.

Their golden days in Venice came as a revelation. Miranda knew she was living a fairy tale. Even her ambitions seemed fuzzy, such was her emotional awakening. There was only Corin. The shimmer and heat of summer. A backdrop of the most beautiful and mysterious city in the world with its grand canal and streets of water.

The flight back to London came much too quickly. Reality set in, as it inevitably did. Already she was steeling herself to face Corin's impending departure for Australia. After which he had a follow-up trip to Beijing to meet up with his father. So separation from this man she had fallen passionately in love with would be her fate.

For long months? Or something far more permanent?

Zara had been home for several hours when they arrived. "Well, you two! Talk about secrets!" She greeted them with open arms, her great dark eyes alight with pleasure and more than a touch of mischief.

Corin had texted his sister, informing her he had taken

Miranda to Venice for the long weekend, and given her an approximate time when they would be arriving home. Now Miranda thought an apology was in order. "Zara, I must tell you I never had the faintest idea Corin was coming to London," she explained. "And I didn't tell you about my birthday because—"

"You thought I'd want to arrange something and bow out of my trip?"

"Exactly." Miranda smiled. "Anyway, now you know. I've come of age. I've had the most breathtaking time!"

"I can see that!" Zara turned to search her brother's handsome face. He was tanned an even dark gold. She had never seen him look more stunning or so vibrantly alive. She had long since formed the opinion Corin had a very special interest in Ms Miranda Thornton, though she had intuited there had been no romantic involvement.

Until now.

Body language expressed so much: love, hate, joy, sorrow, pity, contempt. In this case it expressed the heart. The two of them had that magic aura—the extraordinarily attractive intensity that drew a circle around them and caught the beholder's eye with pleasure, nostalgia or just plain envy. For her part Zara prayed that each had truly found a soul mate in the other. God knew she had forfeited *her* chance at lasting happiness years ago, back home in Australia. But that was another story. She never talked about it, even to Corin. It was buried under many layers.

Already she was very fond of Miranda. One couldn't ask for a sweeter, more harmonious sister-in-law. Could it possibly happen? Miranda was almost eight years younger than Corin, but with an impressive maturity of her own. Corin had huge responsibilites, especially for so young a man. And they would only increase. Miranda had set her sights firmly on becoming a doctor. She knew Corin would support her all the way. Two clever, ambitious people.

But alas, there was their all-powerful, all-interfering father to contend with. At least he loved Corin. He did not love her. She had long accepted that. She had been forced to cope with all the pain and personal havoc her father had caused. Internalise it. Her father, even if he didn't love her, had made it his business to rule her life. He had deliberately altered its course, going out of his way to destroy her chance at happiness with the young man she had loved with all her heart.

Garrick Rylance. A kinsman.

Why had her father done it? He had nothing against Garrick, had he? Garrick was a splendid young man by anyone's reckoning. Yet her father had taken all necessary steps to sever their relationship. Didn't he *want* her to be happy? He had stoutly maintained that wasn't the reason for his ordering her home from Cooranga, the ancestral home of the Rylance cattle barons. Threats would have been more like it. He father was good at threatening people. Perhaps it was her strong resemblance to their dead mother that had closed her out of his affection. His twisted sense of guilt? Whatever it was, she had lived on the periphery. But she had always had her brother as her champion. Yet from time to time the love and pride their father felt for his brilliant son was heavily overlaid by a species of jealousy. A competitiveness. The old lion and the young lion, just waiting to take over the pride.

She couldn't bear to think how their father would react if he thought for one moment that Leila had romantic daydreams about his son. He would probably kill her. Their father was a man of very strong passions. Worse, he had been rich and powerful for so long he acted like a man who was a law unto himself. Despite his children's aversion to his second wife, their father was still deeply in love or lust or both with her. She had dazzled and hypnotised him. Leila—the omnipresent figure who excelled at manipulation.

To Zara's acutely sensitive eye Leila had shown every sign of being secretly infatuated with Corin. God help her if their father ever stumbled on to it. But Leila was smart. And she would do everything in her power to undermine any young woman who sought to play a key role in Corin's life. She had done it in the past. As highly intelligent as Miranda was, she would be a mere innocent in competition with a feline mastermind. If the relationship continued at this level Miranda would have to be told the risks. Leila Rylance was a dangerous woman. Miranda would never have had contact with such a woman in her entire life.

Or so Zara thought.

Corin took them out to dinner. A quiet but exclusive restaurant where they were well-known and their privacy was protected. There was always some member of staff on hand to report that paparazzi were out at the front, looking for some celebrity or other. In that way, if they had to, they could leave by the back door.

Zara spoke of her trip over dinner, telling them a little of her group's dealings and her meeting with a certain high-ranking businessman of renowned wealth: Konrad Hartmann.

"Hartmann? Heard of him, of course." Corin was frowning hard, as though what he had heard wasn't good.

Zara confided, rather diffidently for such a beautiful woman, that Hartmann had taken quite a shine to her. Twice divorced, in his mid-forties, he was a man who enjoyed enormous prestige, but her boss, Sir Marcus, who had a legendary "nose" about these things, was concerned about where all the mountains of money were coming from. So far Hartmann—and he was under close observation—was clean.

"He wants to see me when he comes to London," Zara told them with a faint flush.

"And will you see him?" Corin asked crisply.

Zara took another sip of her wine. "Probably not." A hesitation, then, "He's a very attractive man."

"Better listen to Sir Marcus," Corin clipped off.

Miranda took note of Corin's formidable expression. She knew he was very protective of his sister. "You're a beautiful woman, Zara," Corin said. "You can have anyone you want. One time I thought— Anyway that's another story." He broke off as though on dangerous ground. "Look, this guy might appear up front, but with all that unexplained wealth he's uncharted territory. I'll have him checked out more thoroughly."

"You won't find anything." Zara shook her head. "No one can up to date. And they're looking. It's just one of Sir Marcus's hunches."

"Sir Marcus Boyle is renowned for his hunches," Corin said.

"But you felt an attraction?" Miranda intervened. She knew by now Zara could indeed take her pick of any number of highly eligible men on the social scene. Yet she had taken no more than a passing interest in any of them. Her heart didn't appear to be in it. Miranda was certain Zara had her secrets as well.

The flush still stained Zara's magnolia cheeks. "I did, I suppose. I'm used to powerful men. At the same time it was a bit threatening."

"I think I know what you mean," said Miranda.

Corin's brilliant dark eyes swept over her. She looked radiant, her colouring—the silver gilt hair and turquoise eyes—a wonderful foil for Zara's sable hair and huge dark eyes. To think he had such an intimate tactile knowledge of her body! It was something he regarded as a revelation. "So who has threatened you?" He gave her his fullest attention.

"What if I said *you*?"

"*Me?* Threaten you?" He fell back in disbelief.

"Well, you *are* a member of an important family." She hastened to explain. "You're Corin Rylance, your father's heir. It's easy for the rich not to touch base with ordinary folk like me. Financial worries hound a lot of people to death. You've always been rich. You've probably never even caught a bus."

"I beg your pardon! If I didn't know you better, Miranda, I'd think that was a cheap shot."

"Not at all. A plain statement of fact. Throw in a train."

Corin gave a wry laugh, but Zara looked at Miranda with understanding. "I was the one who went to and from school in the Rolls."

Corin drew Miranda's gaze with the power of his own. "I have caught a bus, Miranda. I can't say a train. The school bus used to take our teams off to cricket, football, swimming carnivals and the like."

"Just tongue in cheek." Miranda smiled. "So don't look so affronted." She had good reason to know by now the rich really were different. They had their problems. Big problems too. But worry about blowing the budget wasn't one of them.

"I think Miranda means some old-style snobs might perceive a gap in the social pecking order." Zara tried to help Miranda out. She knew for a fact their father had the daughter of one of his biggest and most influential business partners in mind for Corin. Their father always got what he wanted. Split up one of his children from the love of her life. Marry off the other.

"What rot!" Corin said mildly. "You'd fit in anywhere, Miranda. You fit better than anyone I know. Outside my beautiful sister, of course." He reached out to grasp both young women's hands.

"Let's drink to that!" Zara suggested with her lovely smile.

Zara had left only the lights on in the entrance hall when they had left for the restaurant. When they returned by cab, a little over two hours later, the whole house was ablaze.

An apprehensive frisson shuddered the length of Miranda's spine. From the moment they'd got into the cab she had a sense life was about to change. Some *difference* in the air. A disturbance.

Danger lurking.

Maybe she really did have a sixth sense? She couldn't feel the way she did for nothing. A fissure in her happiness was about to open up. Could happiness ever last? She knew she had broken out of the social confines of her life. That itself presented big problems.

"Could it be your father?" she asked Zara, trying to hide her agitation. Where Dalton Rylance was, so too would be her mother.

"I don't know!" Zara made no attempt to hide her own unease. Both stood watching as Corin, leaving the young women behind, swiftly mounted the few steps to the front door to check things out. "I doubt it." Nevertheless her voice wavered. "It's as I told you, Miri. I don't get on well with Leila, though she's convinced my father that is entirely *my* fault. Despite all she's supposedly done to reach out to me I continue to regard her as the enemy. To be honest, I have to admit our relationship was doomed from the start. Father showed no understanding. He blames me. Better me than him. I was never in the right, no matter what I did. If they're here, I don't know why. Leila likes to stay at Claridges when she's in town. I would have thought if they were calling in, however briefly, they would have left a message. That's what has happened in the past."

"Then who else could it be? An intruder wouldn't turn on every light in the house."

"No." Zara took hold of Miranda's hand, as if divining they were in need of mutual support. Indeed, they were acting like a couple of robots, Miranda thought.

What sort of woman is my mother that Zara, a beautiful and accomplished woman, fears her? And Corin loathes her?

Did she have some of her mother in her? God forbid. Was she about to find out? No wonder she felt deeply troubled. How would Zara react when she found out she was Leila's daughter? Not only that, she had deliberately kept that knowledge from her? Okay, she had done as Corin wanted. Would that make a difference to Zara? Or would she feel betrayed by both of them? Zara appeared to have trodden a difficult path in life. Her resemblance to her dead mother was only part of it. There was more. She was sure of it. And that *more* involved her mother. Mistress before stepmother? Deeply disturbing.

"Corin's inside." Zara was gasping in air. Her fingers tightened on Miranda's. "We'd better go in. And to think we were all so happy!"

"It must be them." Miranda firmed up her backbone. She was becoming as protective of Zara as Corin.

Think hard thoughts, Miranda. You're not prepared, but if it's Leila she won't know it's you. Leila abandoned you without a trace of memory. The willed amnesia syndrome. No need to slip away to the basement. Zara needs you.

There was the inner voice again, like a non-stop voice-over.

Corin's tall figure had disappeared into the entrance hall. Out of sight. They began to mount the steps, with no option but to do otherwise. Miranda had already arrived at the most unwelcome conclusion. For some reason Dalton Rylance and Leila were in the house. It belonged to them anyway.

They paused to the left of the top step, just out of sight of anyone inside the marble-tiled entrance hall. "Good chance to see who it is!" Miranda muttered under her breath.

"It's Father and Leila, of course." Zara sounded shattered. Something that wasn't lost on Miranda.

The two of them stood mesmerised as they were made witness to the grand entrance of the beautiful, statuesque woman descending the staircase, calling out Corin's name as she came.

He might as well have been deaf, Miranda thought, because he didn't respond.

Undeterred, the woman threw out pale, slender arms in welcome, much as a famous diva might, supremely confident of herself and her adoring audience. She was dressed in a slinky ankle-length dress, a lovely shade between peach and bronze. It suited her perfectly. Her long, thick superbly styled bronze-coloured hair swirled around her shoulders. Her golden-brown eyes, offset by arching black brows, shimmered in the light from the great chandelier. She looked no more than late twenties.

A good ten years younger than she was.

"So that's Leila!" Miranda had to work hard to suppress a sick combination of rage, shock and an involuntary stomach clenching excitement. This, at long last, was her *mother*. Albeit a personage invented. It didn't seem possible. Yet she herself had set the wheels of fortune in motion. Now she felt not triumph—*I've found her at long last*—but a continuing sense of loss. Leila was a head-turner. No doubt about that. Ultra-glamorous. Streamlined seduction coming off her like a powerful incense.

"Corin, dear!" She spoke in a husky, cultured voice, acquired over time. "What a shock it was to hear you were in London!"

Corin remained where he was, remote, stunningly handsome, keeping his distance. "Shock? How would it be a shock, Leila?" he challenged. "You seem intent on following my movements."

"Well, you *are* my stepson!" A low amused gurgle deep in the throat.

"We should go in," Zara whispered, still rooted to the spot. Both had registered that Corin spoke in his coldest, hardest voice.

"Give it a minute." Miranda held tight to her vulnerable friend. She truly believed Leila had tried to break the young Zara. No female competitors for her husband's time and attention. Least of all one who was the mirror image of his first wife. "I want to see something." Indeed she did. There was a tremendous tension between Corin and the outwardly smiling Leila. She couldn't ignore it.

"She's in love with him," Zara confided in an intensely unhappy voice.

"No question!" All trace of their pleasant evening had been wiped clear. "He must know it at some level."

Of course he does, said the warning voice in Miranda's head. *But he's hidden it from you.*

"He won't *have* it." Zara was adamant. "Do you blame him?"

"It would bring great shame to the family." Miranda stared at the tableau before them. Leila had entered her life. There was no going back.

There she is—your mother. A serial adulteress?

"It would!" Zara breathed.

"Then God knows how it will end." Miranda transferred her gaze from her mother to the man she loved. His tall, handsome figure emanated hostility. But it was a man-woman thing. The two of them were locked in confrontation. Was it possible they had shared some secret moments Corin, at least, was desperate to forget? Miranda turned the burning question over and over in her mind. Here was a very beautiful, seductive woman. Such a woman would always have the advantage over a young man susceptible to a woman's beauty. It didn't bear thinking about. On the other hand, she might never be able to *stop* thinking about it.

Women were lied to all the time. Betrayed. She ought to remember she was no woman of the world. She was twenty-one years old. Leila, on the other hand, was the walking, breathing epitome of ancient wisdom and womanly allure. A born seductress. She shook her head as if to clear it. "Your father is a proud and arrogant man. Not a man to cross."

"Not unless you're tough enough to pick yourself up and put the pieces together again." Zara shuddered. "Few are. Me included. Corin brings the ball right to him. Truth to tell, Father is somewhat in awe of Corin, though he'd rather die than admit it. Our father is profoundly unforgiving. I speak from long experience."

Great wealth appeared to make for dysfunctional families! "Oh, Zara!" Miranda locked a protective arm around Zara's waist. How easy it would be to traumatise a young girl. Especially one who had lost the love and support of her adored mother. "Come on, now," she said bracingly, putting her own fears aside. "Let's get it over. Bring Leila's movie-star efforts to fascinate Corin to an end."

Zara responded with a strangled laugh. Together they *swung* rather than moved quietly into the entrance hall.

Their arrival stopped Leila in mid-flight. She turned from devouring Corin with her golden tigress's eyes to address Zara and whoever it was with her. Perhaps with a few subtly mocking words. Nothing Leila could say would lack a certain sting.

Except it didn't happen that way.

Leila stood transfixed. All colour drained out of her face. *"What—?"* Her voice cracked on the solitary word. She looked pole-axed, robbed of all confidence. Her almond eyes opened wide. Full of *fear*?

"I'm sorry." Zara made a little perplexed gesture, looking swiftly to her silent brother for guidance. "This is Miranda—a friend of ours, Leila. We've all been out to dinner. Miranda, this is my stepmother, Leila Rylance."

Pull out all the stops, Miranda. You've served a long apprenticeship. You can do it. You can cope.

Her inner voice came through, unusually fierce. It was beginning to sound more and more like her grandmother. So many currents in the sea of life! Miranda stepped forward, an enchantingly pretty young woman, with exquisite colouring, wearing a short fuchsia silk dress. "How do you do, Mrs Rylance?" She couldn't for the life of her order up a smile, but she found herself able to speak calmly, politely. A well brought up young woman.

Hang tough. This is your mother and she's only a few feet away. The closest she has been in twenty-one long years.

Leila for her part seemed totally incapable of finding her usual brilliant smile. She might have been looking at an apparition, and a nightmare at that.

"Leila, you've gone very pale." Corin's words were solicitous enough, but his tone was far from warm. "Are you all right?"

Leila didn't answer. She backed away, grasping behind her for the scrolled end of the balustrade. When her long, elegant fingers, flashing a fortune in diamonds, found it, she gripped it tight. Consummate actress that she was, she couldn't collect herself, though she was clearly involved in some extremely harrowing thought processes.

"The long trip, I expect," Zara offered kindly, because kind was the way she was, trying to fill in the gap. Leila was feeling unwell for some reason. *No.* That wasn't it. Leila, always in command of herself, appeared to have gone into extreme shock. Zara had no idea why. She had now taken to hugging her bare arms, as though the air had turned icy. How extraordinary! Something to do with Miranda? Zara cast about for a reason, however unlikely.

Corin and Miranda had no doubts whatsoever. Whoever Leila was seeing, it wasn't Miranda. It was Leila's girlhood lover. The father of her child. The child she had been desperate to leave behind. As if she had never been born.

This could be my first meeting and my last, Miranda thought somberly.

So here I am, Mother dear. A threat. Only I don't propose to threaten you at all. Your life is your life. I won't disturb it. My life is mine.

Corin was making some comment when a deep, markedly authoritative voice called from the gallery. The voice of a dictator, a tyrant. One who must be obeyed. "So they're home at last, are they?"

Ah! The magnate billionaire was in their midst.

You don't bother me at all.

Miranda had to wonder why she felt like that. Very many people went in fear and trepidation of Dalton Rylance. It was common knowledge. There was no such fear in her. Her mother *knew* her. Knew her instantly. How elemental was that?

At the sound of her husband's dark, sonorous tones Leila made a supreme effort to pull herself together. Perhaps before it was too late? It had to be an ongoing ordeal, getting into bed with one man while longing for another, Miranda thought without pity. Keeping it from an adoring, jealous husband would stretch the nerves to breaking point, surely?

"They have a young friend with them, darling," Leila called, though her voice, compared to the way Miranda had first heard her speak, sounded thin and weak. Not the voice of a practised seductress at all.

Dalton Rylance appeared at the top of the stairs, an imposing figure in evening dress. He was very tall, very fit, still an extremely handsome man in his late fifties, with a thick dark plume of hair, silver wings, penetrating light blue eyes. He didn't ask for a name. His entire focus was on his wife. "Is anything wrong, my darling?" In an instant he had reacted to the reedy sound in his wife's voice.

If anyone upsets my wife, I'll destroy them.

He might as well have shouted it aloud, Miranda thought. No wonder sensitive Zara trod warily with this man. He might be her father, but he wasn't her friend, let alone her protector. Miranda took a violent dislike to Dalton Rylance on the spot.

"Why would anything be wrong, Dad?" Corin lifted his head, his voice very smooth and self-assured. Corin obviously didn't share his sister's qualms. But then, Corin was the heir. "Leila was just saying she's a little tired from travelling."

"My dear, why didn't you tell me?" Quickly, as though he were at fault, Dalton Rylance descended the staircase. Obviously in thrall to her, he went to his wife's side, staring with great concern into her exotic face, at her golden-olive complexion turned to parchment.

Immediately, no doubt for cover, Leila held a hand to her temple, as though to contain the pain. "I don't like to worry you, darling. You know that. I've been perfectly all right up until now. But it seems to have hit me all at once." Suddenly she sounded very sober. And dangerous. A tigress under threat.

"Then we'll go back to the hotel immediately." A deep frown creased the area between Dalton Rylance's black brows. He pressed his greatest treasure—his wife—against his side. Only then did he notice Miranda.

"Friend of Zara's are you, young lady?" He shot the question at her, giving her a comprehensive once-over. Then, miracle of miracles, he smiled. A very attractive white smile that highlighted the strong resemblance between father and son. Dalton Rylance obviously had quite an eye for a pretty woman.

"Miranda Graham, Mr Rylance." Swiftly she improvised. To say *Thornton* would have confirmed Leila's worst fears. The nightmare of her past was here to haunt her. Most probably to blackmail her. People had been killed for less. "It's an honour to meet you, sir." Graham was her grandfather's Christian name. It was the best she could do on the run. Out of the corner of her eye she saw Zara's head turn wonderingly towards her, but mercifully Zara said nothing.

"We must meet again when my wife is feeling more like herself," Dalton Rylance promised, his manner turned suave. Miranda had very obviously passed muster. "We only popped in for a few moments to say hello. It was Leila's idea, actually, to have a few days in London. Didn't intend it at all. Quite out of the way. But naturally Leila wanted to catch up with Corin and Zara. She's a very caring woman."

Wouldn't it be great to put him straight?

"I'll call a cab for you, Dad." Corin had already pulled his mobile out of a pocket, dialling the number.

"Thank you, son." Dalton Rylance turned belatedly to his only daughter. "How are you, Zara?" There was a terse edge to his tone. To Miranda's ears it was almost as though he felt *obliged* to speak to Zara—something he preferred not to do. She had rejected his darling wife, for a start. Dalton Rylance from all accounts had only become isolated from his daughter since the untimely death of his first wife, his children's mother—or perhaps from the moment it became apparent to his very perceptive children that Leila was a cunning and ambitious young woman who would stop at nothing in her determined pursuit of their father. Certainly their mother had seen Leila for what she was. A woman consumed by the desire for wealth and social status.

"I'm fine, thank you, Father," Zara answered composedly. Zara the classic beauty. A young woman of charm, understanding and high intelligence. In short, a daughter any man would be proud of. Yet here was a man who fended such a daughter off.

"That's all right, then," he huffed. "Getting along well enough with Boyle? No problems?" He turned back to his wife, as though uninterested in the answer. A wife counted far more than a daughter.

"Sir Marcus thinks the world of her," Corin broke in suavely. "Cab's on the way, Dad. You'll be back to the hotel in no time. A good night's rest will help enormously, Leila." He addressed his stepmother, his brilliant gaze black, fathomless. "We all hope so."

How could his father miss the lick of sarcasm?

Miranda was beset by anxiety, but oddly enough Dalton Rylance took his son's words at face value. "My angel!" He bent to kiss the top of his wife's golden-brown head. "Come with me, now. Corin's right. It's sleep you need, dearest girl."

One had to hand it to Leila, her daughter thought. She was making a phenomenal recovery, though her cheeks were still colourless. "We'll catch up," she assured them all sweetly, with a brave little wave of her hand. But her gaze hit on Miranda with the force of a bullet. A warning Miranda was smart enough to catch. Leila, her long-lost mother, pretty much wanted her dead. "I didn't see any of your things lying around, Miranda?" Leila delivered another bullet sheathed in velvet.

So she's been poking around? Checking in rooms. Despicable.

Mercifully, not even Zara had the key to Corin's apartment. Otherwise Leila would have been down there like a shot.

"I'm very neat, Mrs Rylance," said Miranda. "I hope you have a restful night."

"I will. I have my darling husband." Leila lifted her head to bestow on Dalton Rylance a shimmering, conspiratorial smile.

Obviously sex was on the agenda. Leila had to be terribly good at it. Here was a man dazzled on the outside, without bothering to get to know the woman on the inside.

Corin closed the front door, then leaned back against it, releasing a long drawn-out breath. "Damn, damn, damn!" He spat out the words, as though choking on his feelings. The cab had left, taking his father and Leila back to their hotel.

"My angel? Dearest girl?" Miranda questioned with some irony. If proof were ever needed, it was evident one of the toughest businessmen in the world was putty in Leila's hands.

"And who are *you*, dearest girl?" There was a catch of laughter in Zara's voice, but an edge of perplexity too. "Miranda *Graham*?"

"I'll be darned if I know why I said it." Miranda stalled for time, the muscles of her stomach badly knotted. "Motive unclear." Zara was no fool. This looked very much like crunch time.

"You didn't want them to know who you are?" Zara looked at her searchingly. "That's it, isn't it? We saw Leila when she was talking to Corin. She was herself—the *femme fatale*, absolutely secure in her powers. But as soon as she spotted you she turned into a totally different women. It had to be *you*, Miri. The sight of you stunned her. I thought she was going to pass out."

Miranda looked pointedly at Corin, who shrugged, his brilliant dark eyes full of a simmering anger. "I just want to know who the mole is back home. Someone who passes on my itinerary. Work itinerary, that is. Whoever it is, they're sacked. Let's go into the drawing room."

Zara took Miranda's arm. "There's something you two are keeping from me? I knew it. What is it?"

"Sit down, both of you," Corin said, though he remained standing, the dominant figure, obviously tense.

And now you're going to lose Zara. Most probably the two of them. You don't belong here. Leila has seen to that.

Zara was watching her brother very closely now. "You didn't know Father was coming to London?"

"Zara." He groaned. "Do you honestly believe I wouldn't warn you? Of course I didn't know."

"I'm sorry," Zara apologised. "It's just that woman upsets me so. I'm perfectly all right when I'm fourteen thousand miles away from her. She's turned Father against me. For all we know she drove our beautiful mother—"

"I don't see that, Zara." Corin stopped his sister from saying more. "I *have* been keeping something from you. But it was to protect you. I didn't know how you would handle it then. I don't know *now*."

"Oh, God, Corin. Tell me," Zara begged. "It has something to do with Miri, doesn't it?"

Miranda thought it high time she spoke up for herself. *Take what comes on the chin.*

"Leila and I are related, Zara," she said.

Zara almost jumped out of her skin. "Related? In what way?" Her great eyes locked onto Miranda's. "I can't think of anyone less like Leila than you."

"Thank God for that!" Miranda said gratefully. "I have no official standing in your stepmother's eyes. She doesn't know me. You know I've become very fond of you, Zara. You've been so kind to me. I look on you as a close friend. Someone I can turn to. It hasn't been easy keeping my story to myself. You must believe that. I don't think I could bear it if you didn't."

"Let me tell it, Miranda," Corin said, coming to sit beside her. "Miranda has only been following orders, Zara," he explained. "My orders."

Is following orders a valid excuse? Miranda now asked herself.

"I intended to pick the right time," Corin explained, "but Leila showing up like that tonight—you're quite right. She believes herself all-powerful. Dad backs her in everything she does and wants. Now she's pulled the rug out from under our feet. But she didn't get off scot-free. She's been administered one almighty shock."

"I *saw* that, Corin." Zara matched his terseness. "Move on."

Again Miranda intervened. She was her own person. She should speak for herself. "I'm sorry you had to learn it like this, Zara, but Leila is…no easy way to say it, so here it is…my *mother*."

Zara blanched. She shook her head in seeming bewilderment, then jumped up, looking in a stricken fashion to her brother. "*Mother?* Did Miri really say that, Corin? Did I hear right? Leila, our stepmother, is Miranda's *mother*?"

So much depends on how Zara takes this.

"Please don't upset yourself, Zara," Corin begged his

sister quietly. "Miranda didn't even know herself until a few years back."

"*Years?*" Zara's voice soared. She looked at them both, obviously incredulous and deeply distressed they had kept such a thing from her.

"I was brought up by my grandparents, believing them to be my parents," Miranda explained, desperate for Zara to understand. "I nursed my dying grandmother. That was almost four years ago. Only then did she tell me the true story. My mother abandoned me as an infant. She was only sixteen when she had me. Starting out in life. She didn't want a baby to drag her down."

Zara was all flashing dark eyes. "Dear heaven! This is shocking—*shocking*! So why, on reflection, doesn't it surprise me? Leila had a child. You. Miri." She collapsed into an armchair, shoulders drooping under the weight of this new knowledge. "We've been so *close*, Miri, and you didn't *tell* me."

"I'm sorry." Miranda bowed her head, she too showing her upset. "So sorry. I might have lost you. I could lose you now."

Corin took Miranda's hand in his, tightening his grip. "Miranda did as *I* asked, Zara. Blame me if you want to blame anyone. Miranda was all for telling you, but it wouldn't have done you a bit of good. The knowledge wouldn't have given you any rest. You'd have come out with it some time. And who could blame you? All those years of provocation, of Leila's conniving, her malice, behind the scenes stripping you of Dad's affection. She kept you away. She lied all the time: concocted stories, complained of your stubborn refusal to meet her halfway. What do you suppose would have happened had you known about Miranda and confronted her?"

Zara stared back at him, then gave a wild little laugh. "I'd have *murdered* her, like she murdered our mother."

"No, no, Zara." He felt pain like a twisting knife inside him Whatever he and Zara believed, he wasn't going to lay tha charge against Leila at Miranda's feet. "I'm not having that."

Zara shook her head again, trying to rid herself of shock She realised Corin didn't want to her to go on with her sus picions. Of course she shouldn't have said what she had. Th last thing she wanted to do was add to Miranda's heartbreak

Only Miranda sprang up, as though divining the truth. " can't help my mother, Zara. Any more than you can help you father. We don't get to pick our parents. You can't think I *wan* to talk about this woman? This woman without a heart? I'v only laid eyes on her for the first time tonight. I used to think I could fall from the sky and land on top of her and sh wouldn't acknowledge me. But she *does* know me. We saw the evidence of that tonight. You're shocked? Consider *my* shock. And it hasn't even hit me yet. Leila's whole history is mind-blowing. Far better my grandmother never told me."

Corin responded sharply. "Then you'd never have come into our lives." He rose, drawing Miranda back to the sofa "None of us wants that."

Zara slowly lifted her head, her beautiful face full of a heartbreaking poignancy. "So how *did* you and Corin get to meet?" she asked.

"Pretty much as Miranda told you." Corin regarded his sister with compassion. "She approached me for a Rylance Foundation scholarship. She was a very promising candidate. A top-level student. She explained who she was."

"Not quite true." Miranda decided to intervene. Set the record straight. "Corin is putting the best possible spin on it, Zara. What really happened was that I told him Leila *owed* me. I had already checked her out. Checked out your family. I lay in wait for Corin, more or less cornered him, forced his hand."

"Very enterprising too," said Corin, with the first trace of amusement.

Miranda wasn't to be distracted. "My life's ambition, Zara, is to become a doctor. It's what my grandparents worked so very hard for. They were everything in the world to me, but even they didn't tell me the truth. I have to see it as protection, not betrayal. Just as Corin believes he was protecting you by not telling you what he had learned."

Zara sat motionless, head bent, locked in thought.

Miranda was strong by nature, Corin thought. Zara was far more fragile. Miranda had the priceless advantage of being brought up by loving, dedicated *parents*. He and Zara had experienced more than their share of trauma after their mother's death. He had been scarred to a degree. But never to the same extent as Zara. He was the son, the heir. He was *male*. That made a huge difference. To his father and, sickeningly as it was to turn out, to Leila. His scars had healed over. He was forging ahead in life. So was Zara. Up to a point. It was any additional damage to Zara's psyche that was in the balance. The *wicked stepmother* didn't simply exist in fiction. She made her presence felt the world over.

Miranda hadn't enjoyed being party to keeping the truth from his sister. He was well aware of that. She hadn't refused because she trusted him. That was all-important. Up to date Zara had trusted him too.

But now Zara remained quiet.

Please, oh, please, Zara, don't see it as a betrayal, Miranda prayed.

Second by second dragged on. Miranda counted them with her heartbeats. Then Zara lifted her head, her lustrous dark glance embracing them both. "Start at the beginning," she said.

Some note in her voice calmed Miranda's trembling heart.

CHAPTER FIVE

THEY were in the apartment. Miranda had put distance between herself and Corin, her thoughts chaotic. The realisation that she had actually met her mother was starting to hit punishingly home. It wasn't as though Leila, whatever her regrettable actions in the past, had transformed herself into a loving, caring person. Leopards didn't change their spots. Leila was stuck with hers.

So where did that leave her, Leila's biological daughter? She had studied the history of genetics, the chemistry of the genes. The word *heredity* referred to the way specific characteristics are transmitted from parent to child, from one generation to the other. Now she found herself dreading the thought that there could be traits of Leila lying dormant in her. Traits could express themselves at any time. Or had she escaped the major flaws in Leila's character?

What did Corin think when he looked at her? Did he have nagging concerns at the corner of his mind? Who could blame him if he did? She knew sexually they were in perfect accord. But at some point he had to have fully registered she was Leila's flesh and blood. Leila—his stepmother, the woman he loathed. Was it conceivable he was waiting for something beneath the surface in her to suddenly emerge? Tonight she had seen with her own eyes that Leila lusted after Corin. That was already gnawing away at her. It raised terrible questions. Had Corin at some time been caught in some taboo situation? No one could deny such things did happen when an experienced adult manipulated someone much younger.

Shame could encourage hatred.

Zara, before she had retired to bed, had turned to announce prophetically, "She'll be back. You know that."

"Nothing surer," had been Corin's response.

Corin's greatest concern was to spare Miranda what was to come! Protective strategies had already begun to dominate his mind. Miranda, like his sister, was going into self-protective mode. He empathised with Miranda's powerful experience of the night. Her encounter with her long-lost mother. She had been totally unprepared for such deep emotional upheaval. All things considered, she was handling it remarkably well. It only added to his admiration for her. Miranda had real character.

"Is there any way she could mount some attack on me?" she asked now, holding on to the back of an armchair as if for support. "Undermine me? Pre-warned is pre-armed. Will she get rid of me out of your lives?"

"Over my dead body," Corin countered grimly. "Why are you over there, when I'm *here*?" he questioned tautly. He wanted her in his arms, but her mood was very sombre, warding him off.

Leila was no nice everyday mum. If Leila got so much as a hint he had a romantic interest in Miranda she would immediately turn to formulating ways to separate them. After all, she was mistress of that infamous art form. Though he did everything in his power to block it from his mind, he'd had plenty of experience of Leila's seeing off anyone she saw as competition. Sick as it was, Leila still held hopes she could lure him into her bed. She'd been trying it on for years. Even now she wasn't about to give up. She had no sense of honour. Worse, such was her colossal arrogance she thought she had only to catch him off guard. Arrogance was Leila's defining characteristic.

"What sort of woman *is* my mother that she ties everyone in knots?" Miranda begged of him.

He looked back, brows knotted. "The straight answer? She's a born manipulator. She breaks up families. She's cunning. She's cruel. She'll stop at nothing to get her way. Dad is blind and deaf to all this. He's mad about her."

"That could stop if he ever knew the truth." Miranda saw the strain in Corin.

"I doubt it," he answered crisply. "She would come up with something. Some pathetic story. She wanted to tell him so often, but she loved him so much she couldn't bear to lose his trust. She was so young, et cetera, et cetera… Sixteen. It was rape, of course. Or near enough. Overpowered by a man she knew and trusted. Her parents agreed to take her baby and rear it. She sent them all the money she could raise for years. Oh, she's *good*, Miranda. Don't underestimate her. Already she'll be working on her case."

"I don't intend to inform on her. I must make that plain. I thought I would hate her, but in a way I feel sorry for her."

"You *won't*," Corin predicted bluntly. "I can guarantee that. Are you going to come here? Sit with me?" How many times would he have to tell her she was the best thing that had ever happened to him?

"I think better over here," she said with a shake of the head. "It's all changed, hasn't it, Corin?" She lamented. "Simple and sad as that. Our golden days, our *stolen* days, are over. I'll never forget them. But we're back to *real* life. The way things actually *are*. I confess I'm disappointed in you. I never thought I would be. It really hurts."

"Hurts?" That stung him. Purposefully he closed the distance between them. Loomed tall over her. "You think I should have told Zara?" He took her by the shoulders. "You don't know how badly traumatised Zara was as a young girl. She's fought out of it, but a big reason for that is having Leila out of her life."

"All right. I accept that." She stared up at him, seeing the muscle working along his chiselled jawline. "I can see how it happened with Zara and with *you*. I don't want to read more into this than I *saw*, Corin, but I watched you and Leila together tonight. I'm not stupid. I'm a trained observer. You *know* she's in love with you. Why do you deny it? It couldn't be more obvious."

"Well, it's not *obvious* to me," Corin exploded, sick to death of the noxious Leila. "Leila does the big come-on on rare occasions when we're alone. If Dad caught her at it, God knows what would happen."

"Take a guess," she lashed out. At Corin! But she *loved* him.

No matter what?

"Would he throw her out?" she suggested, with a forced little laugh. "Alternatively, would he throw *you* out? God, it could all end in tragedy. At the very least a huge scandal."

"And you think I don't *know* that?" Corin rasped. "Zara knows it. Leila knows it, but doesn't seem to care. Now *you* know. For the record, I'd never for a single second think you stupid. You're as smart as they come. Incidentally, Dad *can't* throw me out. Zara and I have our mother's shares, and my grandparents stand very strongly behind me. Even Dad can't risk that sort of internal fight. Besides, I have the backing of the board. I'm regarded as top man to replace Dad. My position in that regard is quite safe. Dad *needs* me. Our investors are happy dealing with me if Dad is not around. I'm his Number One man."

"And it would appear you're also Leila's Number One man," Miranda said with a trenchancy that shocked her.

His glittering regard gave fair warning. "Don't talk like that, Miranda. I don't like it."

"I don't like it either." She threw up her head in challenge. "Leila has already tried something on, hasn't she?"

No, no, no. Don't let it be true.

Corin's handsome features tightened into a mask. "Miranda, please accept once and for all I have no tender feelings for Leila."

"But I'm not talking about *tender* feelings," Miranda said very crisply. "Leila is one dangerous, over-sexed woman."

"No argument there. But to put it bluntly I *loathe* her. She's a viper. She did her best to cripple my mother emotionally. She succeeded in alienating my beautiful sister from Dad. But, as you so correctly identified, Leila *is* a very sexual person."

"So are *you*!" It was out before she could call it back.

"And so are *you*," he retaliated, his hands tightening on her shoulders. "Maybe I'd better remind you." He took her face between his hands, held it still, then kissed her hard, like a brand. "I want to lead you to bed. I want to make love to you for the rest of the night. Instead we're embroiled in an unsavoury family drama. Leila wants what she *can't* have. Some people are like that. The chase is everything. She went after Dad. She got him. Only he wasn't enough for her. As the years passed, she turned her attention to me."

She tried to break away, but he wouldn't allow it. "Well, it would have been a temptation, wouldn't it? You would have been remarkable even then. A brilliant, sexy young man. I'm sorry if I'm making you angry, but I want the truth. I need it. Maybe it was all a grand illusion, but we've been as close as two people can be. That doesn't mean I believed it was going to last. Or be *allowed* to last. We control nothing in life. We just think we do. This woman, this catalyst in our midst, is my *mother*. There's no physical resemblance. She's much taller than I am. More lavishly built. Her colouring is totally different. I have to be the living image of my father or someone in my father's family. Someone with *my* distinctive colouring. The resemblance is so strong Leila recognised me immediately. She probably thinks I'm up to something. A go-getter like her? Who knows? I could have some of her characteristics in me, just waiting to break out. Ever thought of that?" She held his eyes.

"You're *nothing* like Leila." His black eyes smouldered in his dynamic face.

"Maybe you've only seen me at my best?"

"Don't do this to yourself, Miranda," he said. "Leila is a one-off. Meeting her tonight, so unprepared, has been a big shock for you."

"More than a shock, Corin," she said. A torrent of emotions was racing through her. "Have you ever slept with her?"

"What?" Corin's expression turned very daunting. "I can't believe you said that!" He held her so tightly she winced. Instantly his grip relaxed. "I'm going to *forget* you said that."

"But you *can't* forget." Her beautiful blue-green eyes glittered with unshed tears. "You'll always think of it now. I asked the question. Perhaps you might consider I have a right to. *Have* you?"

"Don't cry. *Don't*." He wiped a tear clear of her luminous cheek. "This is the last time I'm going to say it. I loathe Leila."

"You *could* very easily loathe her. That's perfectly understandable. She tempted you against your will. It might have been years back. She's seductive enough to make the head of a male of any age swim."

"Never *mine*!" He released her as though all his former feelings for her were dissolving. "I adored my mother. There's a sacred principle involved here, Miranda. A son's love for his mother. My mother didn't deliberately leave us. She loved us too much. When her car went flying off the Westlake Bridge, it was at a time when she was in terrible distress. She was at the wheel of a powerful car. Perhaps blinded by tears. She really did love my father. Then she had to confront the fact he had fallen in love with another woman, many years younger. He had brought her into the house. Forced her upon us all. His mistress. I'm sure she was. Even then. When I was seventeen, nearly eighteen—" an unmistakable note of outrage entered his voice "—Leila came to my room. Dad hadn't arrived home. They were going to a party. She needed someone to fix the zipper on her evening dress. Zara was just down the hall. But she wanted *me*."

"Of course she did!" Miranda released a long shuddering breath.

He'll hate you for making him remember. He'll hate you for making him recount an ugly, disturbing incident.

"You needn't go on if you don't want to."

His brief laugh cut her off. "You *wanted* to know, didn't you? Kindly let me finish. Weigh up the evidence, Miranda, before you sit in judgment."

"I'm *not* judging you," she protested. "I can understand this, Corin. I've *seen* Leila in action."

"You *are* judging me," he corrected flatly. "I can see it in your eyes. Eyes are the windows of the soul. So don't back away from it. You started this. Let me finish it. I have nothing to feel guilty about in relation to Leila. She engineered it so her dress—a slip of satin—all but fell from her. Her breasts were uncovered. She wasn't wearing a bra. Most of her body was exposed. I was supposed to be turned on. Instant arousal. Instant disgust, more like. I was supposed to be the callow boy, about to lose control. But she had it all wrong. Even without my love for my mother, my aversion to Leila, I would never betray my father. The whole situation was appalling. I remember yelling at her to get out. *Get out! Get out!* She wasn't such a fool she didn't pull up her dress and make a bolt back to her bedroom. *Their* bedroom—the master suite."

"And that was the only time?" Miranda wasn't shocked. She had *seen* her mother the sexual predator, seen the overweening confidence in the way she stood. Head up, back arched, hand on hip. She'd probably seduced the man who had fathered her. Not the other way around. Her grandmother had admitted Leila had been very *mature* for her years.

Mature? One could define maturity in a number of ways.

"Need I say more?" Corin spoke coldly, as though deeply disappointed in her and her reactions.

"But she hasn't let you alone, has she?" Miranda persisted.

"Okay, let's have this out," Corin retorted in an abrasive voice. "Leila is an extraordinary woman. A man-eater. A home-wrecker. She's very motivated."

"Like me?"

"Let me finish." He cut her off. "Leila thinks sooner or later it's going to happen. She and I *will* eventually have sex."

"Instead it happened with *us*." Solid ground had turned to shifting sand. "Some of that loathing has to wash up on me? If not now at some future time?"

"Now you really are being ridiculous. And unforgivably insulting," he said. "Both to me and to yourself."

"So I should be disgusted with myself?" Miranda asked, low-voiced. "Well, I feel like I'm being pulled apart, Corin. Try to understand that. I *am* my mother's daughter. There's a lot of twisted emotion going on here. In you. In me. Even in Zara."

He rounded on her. "Don't get into the psychobabble, Miranda. Where has our sense of *belonging*, our depth and balance gone?"

"No psychobabble," Miranda said sadly. "A conclusion based on hard evidence. I take the scientific approach. Leila has badly affected your family. Affected me, the abandoned child. We all bear testament to that. She's that kind of woman."

"Ah, to hell with her!" Corin threw up his hands. "We lose the good people in life. The devil looks after his own." What he desperately needed was to hold her, but at that moment it seemed impossible. It was obvious she needed time. As for him—he accepted the fact he had fallen deeply and irrevocably in love with a young woman whose life story was drastically entwined with his own.

But love was a form of armour. Wasn't it? He *had* to believe that.

"If Leila thinks there's anything between us she'll become even more of an enemy," Miranda said. "I think I should go home. Get a job for the rest of the year. I've had almost seven months of luxurious living. I've learned a great deal. I'll never forget it. But it's imperative I keep my feet on the ground. I'll miss Zara, but she has her job and good friends here. You'll be joining your father in Beijing. He'll have Leila with him. So far as she's concerned I'm *Zara's* friend. Which I desperately hope I still am." She paused, watching Corin slump dejectedly into an armchair. "I should take some of my clothes upstairs. Leave most of them here, if I may. Leila obviously doesn't have a key to your apartment."

"I hope that's not a question?" he shot back, his expression dark and forebiding.

"Don't be angry with me, Corin." She was careful to keep her tone level. "I know she doesn't. If she had, she'd already have checked." She gave a humourless laugh. "I called myself Miranda Graham."

"She wasn't fooled."

"Of course not. At least she knew I wasn't about to bring her immediately unstuck. Your father didn't know her as Leila Thornton?"

"Got it in one. Leila Richardson. That's if he even bothered to look at any documents."

"I would never have taken him for a fool."

"He's obsessed with her," Corin said. "Makes fools of us all. I want you to stay with me tonight, Miranda. We'll take some of your clothes up tomorrow. I suggest you go out for the day. I have a meeting I can't put off in the morning. Otherwise I would. Should go on for hours, then I'll be taken out for the obligatory lunch. But I'll be back no later than 3:00 p.m. Leila will make a rush to get at you. She's probably raised all sorts of possibilities in her mind."

"Blackmail, most probably," Miranda said soberly. "She'll be sure I want to blackmail her. Take her for all she can manage to get from your father. I blackmailed you in a way, didn't I?"

Corin came to his full height—a very formidable young man. He went to her, pulling her tightly into his arms. Hunger, anger, a counter-balancing protectiveness blazed out his eyes. "Let's go to bed," he said roughly, putting his mouth to hers.

Immediately, touch leapt across the barriers between them as if they were of no consequence. The kiss lengthened, deepened. Physically, they were in perfect accord. "We must stick together," he muttered passionately when he lifted his head. "Trust together. If we do, all the Leilas in the world can't hurt us."

At that moment Miranda, fathoms deep in love, believed him.

She wasn't sure exactly why she did it, but Miranda elected to remain in the house the following morning.

Zara looked worried. "I can ring and say I won't be in to work," she offered, thus validating their closeness. "I'll make some excuse. No one will mind. I pull my weight."

"I'm sure you do, but I don't want you to do that, Zara," Miranda said, showing her gratitude for the offer. "Even if Leila does turn up I'll be okay. It's not as though she would physically attack me. She might come off second best if she did. A few of my girlfriends and I undertook a course in self-defence a year or so back. I was the shortest, the slightest and the best of the lot." She laughed at the memory. "For months on campus I was called Mighty Mouse. Besides, this is something deeply personal between us. Leila is the mother who abandoned me. Not only me, but her own mother and father, who never got over her defection. My grandmother spoke about it on her deathbed. This won't be a one-way thing. It works two ways. I'll let Leila tell me her side of the whole sorry story."

"Leila never tells the truth," Zara warned. "If you need me I'm only a phone call away. And Corin will get away from his meeting as soon as he can. You love him, don't you?"

Miranda's beautiful eyes were on fire. "At first sight," she admitted. "It was the most powerful connection of my life. Neither of us ever talked about it. That side of our friendship went unmentioned. I had my degree to get through. Corin was always under pressure. Venice was the happiest time of my life." She paused before adding quietly, "But things change, don't they, Zara? You know that. Therefore I must be prepared."

"Don't you *let* them change!" Zara advised. "I did—to my cost. One day I'll tell you all about it. How I lost the love of my life."

Miranda was sitting in an armchair in the sumptuous drawing room, with its antiques, fine art, glorious chandeliers, gilded mirrors, Aubusson carpet, golden yellow silk drapes falling from the ceiling to floor French windows, when a cab drew to a halt outside.

You knew she'd come.

She had to be channelling her grandmother. That was her voice. She could handle the paranormal now.

She stood up, facing the quiet, leafy crescent, as Leila, dressed in a black-and-white two-piece suit—unmistakably Chanel—emerged from the back seat, turning to pay the driver. She looked up at the grand white stucco building, then walked purposefully towards the short flight of front steps.

Don't forget there's a caged tigress inside.

Miranda believed she was locked into celestial wisdom. She went to the front door, opening it just as Leila was about to press the buzzer.

"Ah, Mrs Rylance. How lovely to see you. This *is* a surprise." Miranda stood back as the much taller Leila swept by her, leaving a delightful trail of Chanel No. 5.

"Where have you come from and why are you here?" Leila bypassed all the niceties. She had control of her voice, but her right hand was clenching and unclenching.

Does she mean to sock you?

"Why don't we go and sit down?" Miranda gestured towards the drawing room.

"Don't tell me what to do in my own home!" Leila shot back in the most hostile voice possible. "Who sent you?"

"I think *I* should be the one asking questions here." Miranda surprised herself with her own calm in the face of a storm.

Courage under fire.

Her grandmother again. She was having a lot to say today. Miranda waited for Leila to be seated before she resumed her armchair by the tall French windows. Who knew? She might have to jump out.

"I repeat—who sent you?" Leila was really angry, her golden-brown eyes lit like a bonfire. "What are you up to?"

"Why don't we cut to the chase?" Miranda suggested. "I know you. You know me. Like any mother and daughter. I assume you're not here to ask my forgiveness?"

Leila looked stunned by Miranda's response and her composure. "What is it you want?"

"Good question." Miranda sat back, finding the whole situation the stuff of fiction. Here was her *mother*. A total stranger.

"Money?" Leila sneered. "It's always money. So just how much is it going to take for you to go away? Not just go away. *Stay* away."

Miranda studied her mother's impeccably made-up face. It had an underlying *scream* behind it. Leila was like a wild animal caught in a trap. But even in the golden light pouring into the room she still looked a good ten years younger than her age. Her long, lustrous hair was arranged in a smooth pleat. Her accessories were perfection. She had lovely legs, an ultra-slim, ultra-toned body.

"Gran loved you to the end," Miranda told her in a saddened voice. "You can't even ask about her. Or your father. Gran died a very painful death. Cancer. My grandfather preceded her by a few months. Lovely man—so gentle and kind. Both of them scrimping and saving to provide the best for me. You really deserve to be exposed, Leila. Afterwards there was just Gran and me, although I called her *Mum* all my life. I thought I was a change-of-life baby, you see. You might redeem yourself in a very small way if you told me the name of my father. Clearly you've never forgotten him. I must be his spitting image."

Leila's face froze. And it wasn't due to Botox. She didn't answer for a minute. "You have no father. He abandoned me."

Miranda followed her instincts. She didn't wait for the celestial voice to break in. "I don't believe that for a minute. Maybe you never told him you were pregnant. Maybe you told him you were on the pill. Maybe you went very privately to his parents—mother most likely. Some mothers will do anything for their sons. His mother—my grandmother, God help me—paid you to get out of town. She wasn't going to have her son's life destroyed. How am I doing so far?"

"You could hardly do better." Leila gave her a mirthless smile. "I wasn't good enough to become part of *that* family, my dear. We're lower class, you see. Farming stock as opposed to big sheep station owners. Therefore I didn't belong in one of the richest families in New Zealand. A family that had produced the country's best doctors and academics as well. I was nothing and nobody. She made that very clear. I waited too long to abort you. I was forced to go through with it. If you must know, your father is dead."

That touched a deep, sensitive nerve. The pain was intense. "May I ask how?" Miranda asked quietly.

Leila shrugged an elegant shoulder. "The last time I saw him he was the picture of health. Killed in a skiing accident years later. A mountain of snow got dumped on him, poor man. Can't say I was sorry to read it."

True or false? You have to find out.

"Did you feel anything at all for him, or was it just another sexual thrill?" Miranda asked on impulse.

Leila made a small grimace. "Come on—it was a lifetime ago."

"And haven't you moved on! Could I have a name, please?"

Leila gave her a look sharp enough to cut to the bone. "Don't even *think* of looking the family up. They won't want to know you any more than they wanted to know me. Your grandfather is a big-time professor. Revered."

"Well, then, it will be easy enough to track him down from what you've already told me."

"More fool you!" Leila said scornfully, her face if not her voice tightly controlled. This was a woman never stricken by remorse. A woman who would never admit to the gravest mistakes. "Take my advice," she said. "Let sleeping dogs lie."

"I'm sure they'll recognise me," Miranda continued, as if Leila hadn't spoken. "The sight of me stupefied *you*."

For a second Leila looked as though she had been hit between the eyes all over again. "Oh, they'll recognise you, all right," she said, sounding more and more furious. "You look just like his sister. And him too, of course. That silver hair and the turquoise eyes. Very few people have eyes like that. I'm pleased in a way that you've turned out so well. That's something that has come on me unawares. Good looks in a woman are a tremendous advantage. But what I have to know before we can talk any deal is this—who put you up to it? It was Zara, wasn't it? You contrived a meeting with her back home. I would have done it. It was no accident of fate. A woman has to take fate into her own hands. It was your heaven-sent opportunity to spill the beans. Get revenge. I'd have played it that way. Zara's your friend, isn't she? Though she's years older. Zara hates me. She'll do anything to damage me with Dalton and…and Corin. She's tried to poison her brother against me. It hasn't worked. Of course she blames me for her saintly mother's death."

Some aspect of Leila was corrupt. "Well, it *did* happen after you became her father's mistress," Miranda came back.

Leila blinked, clearly shocked. "The woman's death had *nothing* to do with me," she cried angrily. "It was an accident. Pure and simple. Dalton was going to divorce her anyway. He fell madly in love with me, you see."

Miranda stared back at her glamorous, youthful-looking mother.

Nothing good can come of this.

Miranda had come to the same conclusion. "Looks like he still is," she said. "But I'm thinking you're not and never have been in love with him?"

Leila's answer was a languid, super-confident drawl. "My dear, you could never convince him of that. Outside of Corin, I'm the only person Dalton does care about."

"Then it sounds like you're a good pair. No heart, either of you. Just a high sex-drive." Miranda's tone was strongly condemnatory.

Leila wasn't in the least perturbed. "Don't, my dear, be fool enough to knock sex. It's all most men think about. I should know. Dalton and I will remain a good pair for as long as it takes." Her smile was very cold. "What I don't understand is what you are doing in London. Got Zara to invite you, I suppose? *Money* is enormously seductive. Even being around it."

There was a lot of truth in that. "Zara and Corin were born to wealth," she said. "You and I weren't. I have none of your illusions or ambitions, Leila. Zara and I *are* friends. I'll be going home soon in any case."

Leila made a derisive sound in her throat. "A whole lot richer, you're hoping. What do you do, exactly? You're very pretty, in a highly individual way, but you're way too short to model."

"Perish the thought! You're not going to believe this, but I'm on my way to becoming a doctor," Miranda said. "I already have my BS. That's Bachelor of Science. Now I need my BM."

Flickers of admiration appeared in Leila's eyes. "Well, good for you!" she said, with as much warmth as she could ever muster.

"Thanks, *Mum*!"

"Spare me." Leila waved a dismissive hand. "I was never cut out to be a mum. But you've turned out better than I thought. Seems it's true, then. Blood will out." She paused, her gaze sharpening. "But where's the money coming from? My poor old mum and dad had nothing."

Miranda's eyes shone with an inner light. "They had nothing when they had *you*. But they worked their fingers to the bone so I could have a first-class education. You'd know nothing about that." Somehow she managed to inject a cool touch of irony. "Actually, I won a scholarship with the Rylance Foundation."

"What?" A dark cloud passed slowly across Leila's face. "Zara has nothing to do with the Foundation. You surely didn't approach *Corin*?" Her lush lips were pressed into a tight line.

"What would be wrong if I did?" Miranda assumed an artless voice and lied. "Zara put forward my name. The rest was easy. I had all the qualifications that were needed."

Leila was putting two and two together, making the inevitable five. "How well *do* you know Corin?" Her voice was a lot harder now. There was a near demonic look in her golden-brown eyes.

"I'm sure I don't need to answer that."

"Don't play games with me, girlie," Leila warned, her voice hinting at impending physical action.

"Who's threatening who here?" Miranda asked, getting ready to defend herself and unafraid. She was still Mighty Mouse and she had her celestial gran on side. "You're the one in the hot seat, Leila. Not me. I should tell you Zara knows you're my mother."

Leila looked as though she was about to faint.

"She had to be told," Miranda said. "She's my friend. We're related in a way, thanks to you. Put your head down and take a few fortifying breaths," she said, feeling pity despite herself. "In, out. In, out. Calm yourself."

For a wonder, Leila obeyed. It took a few moments, then she lifted her head, looking as though all her defences had abruptly been swept away.

"That's better. I don't want to harm you, Leila," Miranda said, knowing it to be true. "I'm not like you, you see. You need have no fear. Zara won't say one word to her father. It's agreed what action is to be taken—if any—will be taken by me. *I* am the victim here. The abandoned child."

Leila gave the queerest laugh. "Suppose I have you killed? It could be arranged. An accident crossing the road…"

"Wouldn't do you a bit of good." Miranda's glance slid over this beautiful woman with sick resignation. "It's all on the record," she improvised. "Anything untoward happens to me, the finger points right at you. So don't talk foolishly. And, incidentally, criminally."

Leila's tight smile was more a sneer. "You think I'm fool enough to trust you? You could change your mind at any time. So could that stepdaughter of mine. So let's come up with a solution. How much?"

A wave of anger swept Miranda, but she didn't allow it to show. "How does ten million sound?"

"Ten million?" Leila sat back grimly, as if she was already deciding on the right hit man.

"That's sterling, of course," Miranda said. "Roughly double in the Aussie dollar. I'd be set up for life. You understand that, don't you, Leila? That would have been your very thought the moment Dalton Rylance's roving eye fell on you. *I can get this man. Be rich!*"

Leila stared back in genuine disbelief. "How could I get hold of that kind of money?"

"Sell a few jewels?" Miranda suggested. "You can't ask your husband. I understand that. We could do it in stages, if you like. The odd million here, a couple of million there..."

"You're *unbelievable*!" Leila spat.

"You astonish me, Mother," Miranda said. "Look at yourself. What *you've* become. My role model. Your husband isn't looking beyond the beautiful face and body. The acquired polish. What happens if and when he does? The most beautiful, seductive women have to age. None of us can escape the process. Once past their use-by date, they're not wanted any more. Some men only want trophy figures, after all."

Leila jerked up in volcanic anger. Outraged. And outflanked. "Cross me and you put your life on the line. You'd better know that."

"At long last I've met my mother," Miranda breathed. "A woman who considers she has never done anything that requires explanation. You broke your loving parents' hearts. You've haunted me, but I've managed to keep my heart intact. No, Mother dear. No need to go back to the hotel and rifle through your little black book for a hit man. I want to make it perfectly clear to you I don't want *anything* from you. So you can sit down again and relax. You have your life. I have mine. I'm not going to simply vanish, like you. I might pop up from time to time. But your former life—the life you've secreted away—is safe with me. Gran saw nothing of you in me. Thank God for that. Most women would find their only child the crowning glory of their life. Not you. It might strike me as shocking, but I accept it. Gran loved you to the end, you know? But she knew in her heart you weren't worth a bumper."

Leila stood for a moment, apparently numb. "I can trust you?"

"Would that be your first experience of trusting? Maybe your husband doesn't trust you? That's why he takes you with him wherever he goes. You *can* trust me. The mother-daughter relationship is a powerful and unbreakable bond. I don't want to see you come a cropper. I'm really not a vengeful person."

Leila stared into her daughter's crystal-clear turquoise eyes. "Don't feel sorry for me, Miranda," she said bitterly. "I have everything I want."

Everything? I don't think so. She wants the man you love.

Point taken, Gran.

Leila appeared to brighten. "Well, that's it, then!" She gathered up her expensive designer bag. No doubt worth thousands of dollars. "I'm taking it Corin knows none of this?"

"*Zara* is my friend," Miranda offered by way of an answer.

"Keep it that way," Leila said. "You're smart enough to realise it would do you no good at all to expose me. Corin and I are close. I would strike back. There are always ways."

Miranda stood up. "You have my word, Leila. On your mother's grave. She wouldn't want me to destroy you. Your life is your own. By and large it always has been. It's never been mine."

Leila started to head towards the door. "Dalton was rather taken with you, in an avuncular sort of way. You're extremely attractive, but you really ought to let your hair grow. He wants to take us all out to dinner before we leave, which is at the end of the week. Both Dalton and Corin have to be in Beijing for a round of business meetings. What say tomorrow evening? You can't refuse."

"Like I don't know that!" Miranda said very dryly. "Could I bring a friend?"

Leila turned, smiling. A real smile. "A boyfriend? Of course you've got one."

"His name is Peter. Australian. He's a brilliant young cellist. I've known him for years. He's studying at the Royal College of Music here in London. He's been assured he has a future."

"Fine, fine," Leila said, putting up a hand to her immaculate hairdo. "Call me a cab, would you? I'm meeting Corin for lunch."

Now that was silly!

Miranda cast off the suspicion.

"Bring your Peter by all means," Leila said, as though a burden had been lifted off her. "I think we'll dine in. We're at Claridges. Wonderful hotel. It suits us perfectly. Even *you* will have heard of Gordon Ramsay's restaurant there."

"We've all heard of Gordon Ramsay, Leila."

"Now, I *can* give you some money, you know," Leila offered. "I guess I owe you that much."

Miranda shook her head. "It's not about money, Leila. I'm going to get ahead. I'm going to become a doctor. Just like my father's family. That's one mystery you've solved."

Leila showed a shadow of concern. "I'm just enough of a mother not to want you to get hurt. Like me. I can't stop you from finding out who they are. I can see you're a very smart girl. But I can warn you to keep well away. Your paternal grandmother, my dear, unlike me, is a total bitch."

Leila sounded as though she truly believed she was basically a good person.

"How old was he? My father?" Miranda asked quietly.

She wasn't showing it, but inside she felt deeply wounded. A father she would never meet. As an individual, she was very short on relations.

"The same age as me," Leila admitted carelessly, as though they were talking ancient history. "He'd never had a girl before. Not that I was a virgin. *He* was. He was head over heels in love with me. Not the only one, I can tell you." She walked to the door, then turned back for a moment. "Until tomorrow evening, then, *Miranda*. Where did Mum rake up *that* name? Blue-green eyes, I suppose. I only saw them as navy. Dress up. Tell your friend black tie."

CHAPTER SIX

AFTER she was gone, Miranda curled back in her chair like a young woman in pain. She felt very strange, as if severely dehydrated. Why not? Leila had all but drained the life out of her. Where was this mystical love that was supposed to exist between mother and child? Certainly her lovely grandmother had loved the daughter who had turned her back on them all to the end. And she, herself, had been the central figure in her grandparents' lives. They had lavished their love on her. They had been so proud of her. Going on the evidence, Leila had no need whatever for any mother-daughter relationship. She had been biologically capable of giving birth. Tragically, she was mentally and morally incapable of nurturing that child. To her, motherhood was only a commitment that dragged a woman down.

Corin arrived back earlier than expected, at 2:30 p.m. She watched him bound towards the front steps, reinforcing the impression he was very anxious to get home to her.

No need to be volunteering information. Let Corin do the talking.

She didn't know at this stage when her inner voice started and her grandmother's stopped.

Because you're part of me. We're part of one another.

Corin was inside now, devastatingly handsome in his elegant city clothes, the pristine white collar of his blue-and-white striped shirt accentuating a deep golden tan that could never came out of a bottle. He drew her into his arms without saying a word. So easy to take refuge. So easy to dissolve into him, to feed off his blazing energy. So easy to suspend deep concern.

He tipped up her face to kiss her, long and lingeringly. "Got away without much trouble," he murmured, when he lifted his head. "I hear you've had a visit from Leila."

She looked directly into his eyes. What was she looking for? Deception from Corin? Leila had really undermined her confidence. "How did you know?"

He reacted to the strain in her voice. "She rang my mobile, of course. What else? Leila lives to alienate people. It would serve you well not to forget that. She sounded super friendly. She's the ultimate con-woman. Seems we're all invited out to dinner tomorrow night. Dad, apparently, took to you. Never could resist a pretty woman."

"When was it she rang you? You didn't see her?"

"Hey, what is this, Miranda?" His tone was different from before. Anger was stirring. "Listen to what I'm saying. I refuse to be put under suspicion. I refuse to have my integrity questioned. I'm an expert at evading Leila. I'd been tied up with the meeting. Which went well, thank you for asking," he added crisply. "She caught me about two minutes before I flagged down a cab. She said you were bringing your boyfriend along. I take it she meant Peter?"

"I don't think Leila would care to hear my boyfriend is *you*." Miranda knew she was on dangerous ground. Throwing down the gauntlet, as it were. But he had to pick it up. "I *was* getting around to asking about your meeting, but my priorities seem to be all screwed up."

He turned her to face him. "So why don't you tell me about them? I'm here now. Peter is a smokescreen. I've got that, although I know you're very fond of him. What did she have to say to you?"

"Actually, *I* did a lot of the talking."

"Which seems to have exhausted you. Are you going to let me in on the conversation?" His dark eyes were trained on her face. It would be a disaster if he lost her trust.

She lifted her head to him, seeing herself reflected in the brilliance of his eyes. "I must repeat I'm not going to expose my mother, Corin. Not for you. Not for anyone. Deep down I think she's a very unhappy, driven person without any real self-esteem."

Corin's hands dropped away. There wasn't just disapproval in his voice, there was outright disgust. "Even if it were true, Miranda, I couldn't care less. She's caused too much harm to my family. She's failed to be any sort of a mother to you. For the record, as it appears I'm under investigation, I don't believe I've ever said I *was* going to expose her."

"So what *do* you intend?" Discord was growing between them like a malignant plant.

"Why sound so ominous?" he challenged. "It means we'll leave it alone. Zara and I care too much about you, Miranda, to override your wishes. You don't want to reveal Leila's history. That's it!"

"You'll keep your word?"

His expression toughened. "With one proviso. Leila must swear not to further upset you or interfere in your life. Should she do that, the position will change. She knows Zara and I know?"

"She thinks only Zara knows. That's all. She did ask if you knew. My answer was ambiguous, but she took it at face value. I told her Zara was my friend."

"So you and I are not supposed to be close?"

She stared back at him, wanting the discord to cease, but unable to stop its escalation. "I played it that way, Corin. Safer, don't you think?"

"Only for a time." There was a brooding expression on his dark, handsome face. "All we have is a breathing space. I won't let you go out of my life, Miranda. You can't think for one moment I will."

She gave a broken laugh. "Well, we *are* related by marriage."

"Oh, stop it!" He drew in a tense, frustrated breath. "Leila has only just arrived on the scene and already she's causing trouble. You can't let her get to you, Miranda. Bad enough she's started to erode your trust in me. There will be difficult times ahead. Leila would like nothing better than to see you out of the way."

"I realise that," she said quietly, averting her head.

"Don't let it weigh you down. Zara and I have had years and years of Leila. You've only had a matter of hours. Yet she's messed up your thinking, hasn't she?"

"Give me time, Corin."

"Of course." He drew her into his arms again, his own expression softening. "Don't let Leila come between us, Miranda," he begged. "She's so good at that sort of thing. I wish I didn't have to leave you, but Dad and I have the China trip."

That was the hardest part. "Leila's going along?"

"She always does," he clipped off.

"She can't want to go all the time—be on her own for hours on end. Doesn't he trust her?"

Corin gave a bitter laugh. "Would you? It's just as well billionaires aren't all that thick on the ground, or Leila would be running off with a younger one."

Her unspoken *like you* hung in the air.

Insight into her thoughts sharpened his tone. "I'm not a billionaire yet, Miranda. I won't be until my father dies, and I want him to last for another twenty-five years. He hasn't been much of a father, but he's all I've got. He does give me due credit as a fitting heir. In his own strange way he loves me. He has need of me as a business confidant. He keeps things so close to his chest, and I'm sure I'm the only one he truly trusts."

"And he has some suitable young woman lined up for you?" Miranda continued to look questioningly at him. "Annette Atwood, isn't it?"

"Are there no limits to gossip?" He sighed. "There's no chance in the world, Miranda. I can't marry a woman I don't love with all my heart. I had thought that was *you*. Now I have to ask. Do you *want* me to love you with all my heart, or does that frighten you? Were our days and nights in Venice just too perfect, too unreal? You can't believe in what we had now you've hit the first obstacle? I refuse point blank to allow a woman like Leila to destroy our relationship."

She stared blindly at a landscape on the wall. "I'm not holding you to anything, Corin. I care too much to bring more trauma into your life. Leila mightn't want to have anything to do with me, but I can never escape being Leila's daughter. It's like a stain."

The melancholy note in her voice pierced his heart. He drew her against him, his arms steely strong, the muscles rigid. "I won't allow you to see it like that," he said forcefully. "You're lovely, inside and out. When you think about it, you escaped your mother. Instead, you were blessed with your grandparents. They brought you up. As for me, I refuse to let you go. You've given yourself to me of your own free will. So I'm keeping you, Miranda. God knows, I've had to resist every temptation so you could get on with your studies undistracted. You have your science degree in your pocket. That's the first step. I'm very proud of you and your sense of commitment. I'll support you every inch of the way in your ambitions. But you're twenty-one now. I want more of you. You've seen Leila. You've felt her destructive power. Don't let her reach you."

"In her way, she's the one who should fear," she said, taking great comfort from his words and his arms around her. "She has so much to hide."

"Indeed she has!" Each word was flattened, as though weighted down. "But don't let's waste any more time talking about Leila. I want to take you shopping."

The dazzling change of topic brought out a flicker of a smile. "Do you really?" She was picturing the two of them together. "I thought men hated shopping?"

"Well, we shopped in Venice, didn't we? You have that beautiful gold-shot glass horse from Murano."

"And I treasure it," Miranda said. "Are you going to tell me what we're shopping for?"

There was unrestrained ardour in his dark eyes. "A dress for you to wear tomorrow night. I want you to knock Dad and our dear Leila dead."

Peter, giddied to be invited, presented very well in a hired dinner suit. He had the height, the wide shoulders, and he had put on much needed weight.

"Peter, you look great!" Miranda reached up to kiss his cheek.

"Bought the dress shirt and the black tie—rented the suit." He grinned. "You look out of this world!" He fell back theatrically, gasping with unfeigned admiration. "If I were wearing my glasses they'd be steamed up. The dress is fabulous! You look a million dollars. Surely they're not *diamonds* dripping off your pretty ears?"

She smiled impishly, fingering one of the diamond-studded drops. "Real, absolutely! On loan from Zara. Come on in. Zara and Corin will be down soon. Both of them are so pleased you're coming along tonight."

"To be honest, I'm blown away to be invited," Peter said, moving farther into the entrance hall and glancing up the grand staircase to the art-lined gallery. "Word is Mrs Rylance is a real knock-out."

"Well, you can make your own mind up."

"Goodness, how intriguing!" Peter looked quickly back at her, but her silver-gilt head was turned away.

Whatever did Miri mean?

To his perfectly tuned ears it sounded as though she hadn't taken to the second Mrs Rylance at all. He reminded himself he had always respected Miri's judgment…

Miranda was glad she had become familiar with the full on dazzle of Claridges black-and-white marble front hall, with its tall mirrors and superb Art Deco ironwork, so her head wasn't swivelling like Peter's. The hall led on to the sumptuous foyer, where she and Zara had enjoyed afternoon tea on several memorable occasions—once when a famous movie star had been seated at a table only a few feet away. She might have been reared on a small farm in rural Queensland, but she was taking the glittering London night life in her stride. This was a time to be enjoyed. A time to capture and relive in memory.

She and Zara had planned their outfits to complement one

another. Like a magician pulling a bouquet of flowers out of a hat, Zara had taken from her wardrobe a deep emerald silk-satin dress with a short sparkly bolero that harmonised beautifully with Miranda's dress, which was the gorgeous shade of a blue-purple iris. The bodice was tiny, strapless, the short, flirty, tiered skirt cinched with a wide satin diamante-clasped belt to show off her enviably small waist.

Beautiful dresses were powerful confidence-builders. Zara, born into wealth, had been wearing beautiful clothes all her life. It was all very recent for Miranda. As a student she'd bought cheap, but her petite figure and inherent good taste had turned cheap into stylish. Her girlfriends had thought so anyway. They had often enlisted her aid—down to actually borrowing an outfit when they were going out on a special date.

Corin had picked the dress out of several, all of them beautiful. His choice had been so wickedly expensive she had tried to talk him out of it. And then there were the accessories to complete the exclusive image!

"It's terribly, terribly *you*, my dear," the saleswoman had told her, looking very expensive and sophisticated herself. She had turned on the charm for Corin from the moment they had walked through the door. And Corin had played up to her, Miranda was sure. He had a streak of devilment.

When Leila first caught sight of Miranda, she gave her the blankest stare—as if in no way had she expected Miranda to look so exquisitely and so expensively turned out.

Miranda now knew with certainty she was looking her absolute best.

She's not happy!

Miranda, who had been lightly holding Peter's hand, as her evening date, felt him squeeze it. Perhaps letting her know a light had been switched on in his head.

It had been. So *this* was the second Mrs Rylance! Peter regarded her, fascinated. A stunning woman, a bit on the dangerous side. Facing down the competition probably dominated her life. Sad, that! He could just imagine her on the rampage. She was wearing black, intricately draped, off the shoulder, showing a generous amount of golden cleavage. Her thick, burnished hair was swept smoothly back from her high forehead and coiled at the back, no doubt to showcase her bedazzling diamond jewellery: earrings like chandeliers, which swung with every movement of her head, and a necklace that danced and glittered with light. It must have set her very imposing magnate husband back millions.

Ah, well, what was a million or two? A billionaire needed a wife who could dazzle. The second Mrs Rylance without question did that.

"What do I do? Bow down on one knee?" Peter whispered, head bent, shoulders hunched, so Miranda could hear him.

"Just hope she likes you."

Was that a warning?

Cocktails were served in the bar, with its deep red leather banquettes and silver-leafed ceiling. Every drink available was on the offer—the classics and the latest concoctions—all served perfectly chilled in crystal. Each table was decorated with a single red rose at its centre, but they found their way over to a reserved banquette.

"Sit here," murmured Corin in Miranda's ear, settling her deftly between him and Peter. Leila, thank the Lord, was busy saying something to his father, so missed the smooth manoeuvre. "I'd suggest a champagne cocktail."

"Lovely!" Miranda smiled, sinking into the seat. She had been extremely careful not to let her eyes rest on Corin over-long. This wasn't the time to invite catastrophe. He looked strikingly handsome, his resemblance to his father apparent. The Rylances were one good-looking family. Zara had to be one of the most beautiful women in a room full of glamorous and beautiful women, Miranda thought.

Dalton Rylance's first act on greeting Miranda had surprised even his children, and brought a glint to Leila's eyes that had been veiled in a second. Even so Peter had caught it, and felt like ducking. Rylance hadn't taken Miranda's small extended hand, as expected, but had bent to kiss her on both cheeks, clearly enjoying the sensation of satiny smooth young skin against his lips.

"You look exquisite, my dear." He straightened, smiling down into her eyes. "Your young man here must be very proud of you."

"Oh, I am, sir!" Peter spoke up, playing his part to the hilt. "And may I say how happy I am to be invited?" He sounded it, but not overwhelmed. Peter, since his exceptional musical gifts had been acknowledged, had come a long way in confidence. Besides, he came from a prominent family back home—though they certainly weren't swimming in the Rylances' ocean of money.

"Good. Good," Dalton Rylance clipped off, his attention not to be diverted from Miranda, who was looking irresistibly young and sexy. He had given his daughter, Zara, just one perfunctory kiss on the cheek.

What an act of kindness!

Playing to the public, of course.

Gran had come along for the evening, apparently having no difficulty in moving between parallel universes.

Miranda couldn't help but be aware that many eyes had strayed in their direction. Dalton Rylance and his ultra-glamorous wife were frequent guests of the hotel, and the small party with him tonight included his strikingly handsome son and his very beautiful daughter, who was a regular on London's social circuit, along with two young guests—all of them a treat for the eye.

The very generously sized restaurant featured more of the Art Deco for which the hotel was famous. Miranda loved the bronze-and-gilt metal doors, the mirrored murals and the lighting. The food was predictably superb, and Dalton Rylance ordered the finest wines to go with the successive courses from the French menu. The hotel had an outstanding cellar. It was being given a real work-out that night.

Miranda was surprised at how much Leila drank, although she didn't appear affected. Zara drank sparingly, but she clearly enjoyed the beautiful wines, as did Miranda. Neither young woman had any intention of matching Leila, or they would have slipped under the table.

The extraordinary thing was, the evening went very well. Dalton Rylance, as host, was in excellent form, as was their hostess, and his clever, sophisticated son carried a good deal of the wide-ranging conversation. Indeed, Leila turned frequently to Corin, smiling, begging him to cap off some story. Family solidarity. Here was a stepmother everyone might long for. But to those who knew her she was playing a role for which any major actress would have taken home an Academy Award. Not once did Leila slip. She laughed. She talked. She revelled in her beauty, power and position of prestige. Such things were what she lived for. It was her destiny.

But beneath the façade Leila Rylance was stewing in a white-hot fury. Practised as she was in concealing her emotions, she was fighting hard to contain them. Now, of all times, the daughter she had given birth to all those years ago had appeared on the scene to *ruin* things. Her daughter's ability to catch her husband's eye was one thing. Nothing could possibly come of that. Dalton had always had an eye for a pretty woman. Only there had been a fleeting moment when she had intercepted a glance between Corin and Miranda.

A split second to a woman like Leila was all it took. It had turned her warm, glowing flesh to ice. Even her vision had darkened. Yet with a tremendous effort of will she'd managed to choke down the shocked gasp in her throat—but not the tidal wave of jealousy. She was forced to sit there, holding down her explosive feelings with all her strength.

Corin had had a number of affairs. They had never lasted. But, to her infinitely keen eye where Corin was concerned, she had accepted in a nano-second that he found Miranda, the daughter she had abandoned, powerfully attractive. She had seen desire in too many men's eyes not to be able to recognise the faintest glint. Corin wanted Miranda. Had he already had her? Of course he had. They were lovers, the devious little bitch. Though God knows didn't that prove Miranda was indeed her child? she thought bitterly. Both of them were born schemers.

With her obsessive mind-set she had convinced herself that one day Corin would surrender to the forbidden attraction between then. The day would come when he allowed himself to be lured into her bed. She lived for it. Her very nature had as its bedrock *sex*. Sex with Corin would be fabulous! It had to be experienced.

The young man Peter was simply a blind. He and Miranda were friends. No more. The young man loved her, of course, but Miranda simply treated him with affection. How different was the relationship between Corin and Miranda! She couldn't miss the depth of desire in Corin's brilliant dark eyes, the fleeting but profoundly revealing response from Miranda. Miranda was head over heels in love with him. Every bit as much in love with him as *she* was.

How had it all happened? When? What was the game they were playing?

She wouldn't tolerate it. It had to be stopped. No way could she allow the glittering life she had built up for herself to fall apart. If anyone was going to get hurt, it wouldn't be her. When the timing was ripe she would expose Miranda as a nasty little blackmailer. *She* had set up the whole thing. Used Corin and Zara for her own ends. It would have to be sooner rather than later. Dalton might be in sexual thrall to her now, but how long was that going to continue? She was in her prime. But even she couldn't hold back the hands of time. Her husband's passion for her would pass. Before that she had to save her own skin.

Corin had booked a limousine for the evening. They were to drop Peter off first, at the flat he shared with three other very promising students from the Royal College.

"She *knows*!" Peter grabbed the opportunity to whisper in Miranda's ear.

The limousine was sliding to a halt a few feet away, Corin and Zara were moving towards it, waiting for them to catch up.

"Knows what?" She spoke sharply, because she had already intuited the answer.

"About you and Corin. The fact you're in love. Tread carefully, Miri," he warned, kissing her cheek. "That's one dangerous woman, in my opinion. How the hell doesn't her husband know?"

"None so blind as those who refuse to see," Miranda answered, very sombrely. "Thank you for being so supportive, Peter. I love you dearly."

"Ditto!" said Peter, flashing her a sympathetic smile.

She and Corin might have Leila Rylance to contend with, but in his view Miranda and Corin would make a wonderful couple. Maybe it was time for him to work on his increasingly friendly relationship with Natalia, one of his flatmates. Natalia Barton was a brilliant young pianist. She had acted on several occasions as his accompanist, and a fine job she had done too. They were very much in harmony—as musicians and as people. Music was to be their lives.

CHAPTER SEVEN

WHEN the three of them arrived home, they all headed into the drawing room to go over the evening's events. Corin mixed himself a single malt Scotch and ice. Zara and Miranda settled for mineral water.

"Do you hate your mother for what she did to you, Miri?" Zara asked presently, setting down her glass on a little giltwood marble-topped table.

"I can't forgive her, Zara, but I don't hate her. I can't forgive her for the terrible hurt and worry she inflicted on my grandparents. She doesn't appear to have any remorse."

"God, no!" Corin agreed bluntly. "Leila doesn't trouble herself with such things. Everything begins and ends with her. She truly believes it was her destiny to have power and money. She must have dreamt about it, hungered after it from girlhood, determined she would get it."

"So what does she say about your father?" Zara asked in her lovely gentle voice.

Miranda's turquoise eyes glittered with inner disturbances. "That he was very young, like her. That she didn't even tell him she was pregnant. He never knew. Now it turns out he's dead," she added starkly. "A skiing accident in New Zealand."

Corin's black brows drew together as he felt a searing stab of hurt. "You could have told me."

"I wasn't hiding anything, Corin." Miranda turned to him quickly, seeing his reaction. "I wanted a little time to take it in myself. It also appears my paternal grandfather is a highly respected medical man."

"Now, why doesn't that surprise me?" he said. "It'll be easy enough now to trace your father's family. That's if you want to?"

"*Do* you want to, Miri, dear?" Zara asked, sadly aware a new tension had arisen between Miranda and her brother. One needn't wonder why. Leila had brought so much unhappiness on them all. Hadn't she felt the virulence in her stepmother all through the evening? The venom behind the practised charm? Miranda wasn't a long-lost daughter. Miranda was a challenger—the stand-in ready to oust the star.

"I don't know, Zara," Miranda confessed. "Leila said they wouldn't want to know me any more than they wanted to know her. It was my father's mother—*my grandmother*—that she spoke to. She was the one who gave Leila money. Some grandmother!" she lamented. "How could she ignore *me*?"

Corin took her hand, soothing the palm with his thumb. "At that time the woman was thinking only of her son and the impact on his life. A lot of mothers are like that. He was very young. He had his whole life in front of him. She wouldn't have allowed him to be burdened with a pregnant girlfriend and a child. It's very possible she has deeply regretted her actions through the years. Especially as her son lost his life."

"So why didn't she try to find me?" Miranda asked, showing painful emotion.

"Maybe secrecy is her creed? Just like Leila." Corin struck a sombre note. "Don't upset yourself, Miranda. It will be easy enough to find out everything you need to know about your paternal grandparents. Only then, I think, will you be in the position to decide what you want to do."

Zara went off to bed a short time later.

"So, what was Peter whispering about?" Corin asked.

Anxiety spiked. "He warned me that Leila *knows*."

"Peter doesn't miss much, does he?" Corin observed dryly, moving about to turn off lights.

"He's very observant. And to think I'd been concentrating on not looking at you for over-long."

"Then Leila intercepted a glance. She has a genius for that." He allowed his gaze to rest on her. "You look wonderful tonight. Small wonder Leila was flooded with jealousy. And you got Dad's attention. He was captivated."

"I don't think that worried Leila." She looked up at him as he stood above her. There was usually such pleasure in studying every aspect of his striking face—broad forehead, high cheekbones, sculpted chin, the brilliance of his dark eyes. Now she felt like a pinned butterfly, unable to withstand that dark scrutiny. She hadn't properly taken on board that Corin was already a powerful personality, and that power would only increase. Right at that moment she felt hopelessly outmatched. Yet she persisted. She needed to push for answers. "She's going with you to China. A lot can happen in a week."

"Like what?" He stared at her, his expression pure challenge.

Now she felt thoroughly flustered. Didn't reply.

"I thought we'd been over this, Miranda." His gaze eased. "What bothers you, exactly?"

Tell him.

"I have this premonition of trouble. So ominous! It makes me feel like I'm lost at sea. I don't know where all of this will ultimately lead. Leila is a powerfully sexual woman. She never stops trying. I'm frightened your father will suddenly whip off his blindfold and see what's been right in front of his eyes."

Corin started to circle the room like a big cat on the prowl. "Then he'll see I have no liking—let alone *love*—for Leila." Miranda's concern, the worry in her eyes, were driving him to strengthen his case. Only *what* case, for God's sake? He had done nothing wrong. But he knew he had to deal with Miranda's fears. She was handling an extraordinary situation remarkably well, but she was clearly in a state of crisis, trying hard to keep her feelings under control.

Leila, the mother she had never known, was suddenly on the scene. A *major* player. Leila, the stepmother for whom he and his sister felt only contempt, the woman who had deliberately gone about destroying his parents' marriage and ultimately their mother's life. He had long divined what was eating away at his father. It was *guilt*. With Zara, a constant reminder, fourteen thousand miles away, his father had been able to shuffle off the burden for much of the time. But many people outside family were still deeply troubled by the way his mother had died.

Miranda's voice brought him out of his tormented thoughts. "I hate liars," she said. "They're such dangerous people. Leila is not unlike a wild animal. If she's cornered, she'll lash out."

"Or move in for the kill." Corin spoke with a contemptuous rasp. "Leila is a stalker. There are women like that. Women who want vengeance for being scorned. Please let me deal with her. Don't forget she has a lot to hide."

"She does indeed," Miranda agreed, quietly intense. "I'm not forgetting anything, Corin. But neither of us can hide from the fact I came out of my mother's body. No matter how dark her journey through life, I don't want to hurt her. She's my *mother*. It's very strange how life works out. I'm not a vindictive person. My ambition is to be a healer. As for Leila, so much depends on just how long your father will remain captive to her. He is at the moment. So Leila could well concoct a story he might well fall for. She could claim I've threatened her with exposure. Demanded money from her. Blackmail, no less. She could be doing it right now for all we know."

He made a very impatient slicing movement with his hand. "Guesswork is tiring and unproductive. I don't like to see you so upset. Come down to the apartment now. I'm sick to death of hearing about Leila. You were so happy, so hopeful. I hate to see that change. No one is happy with Leila around, Miranda. Not even Dad. Our being separated even for a week doesn't sit easily with me," he confessed.

Corin closed the apartment door as if he was closing out the world. "If Leila is going to make some move she'll wait until the Beijing trip is over. I don't think it would be wrong to do some threatening myself." He shrugged out of his dinner jacket, undid the black tie. "It might even be a pleasure. Trying to make Dad see me as someone who desires her would be absolutely crazy, even for Leila. My father *knows* me. He knows better than anyone his children think Leila should burn in hell."

Miranda couldn't prevent a sick moan. "Burn in hell? She's my *mother*, Corin! I feel more pity for her than anger or a thirst for revenge." She went to stand in front of one of Zara's shimmering landscapes, hoping it would calm her. "Do you see anything of her in me?" she turned to ask.

The anguish in her beautiful sparkling eyes made Corin move with swift, unleashed power. He pulled her into a long kiss. Not gentle. A kiss of craving that contained a high degree of emotional frustration. "No, no, a thousand times *no*! I refuse to allow you to distance yourself from me with these worries," he muttered, his mouth still pressed against hers. "Leila erased you from her life. You must do the same to her. I have such *need* for you, Miranda. Can't you feel it? I can't *stand* to be apart. I want to bind you to me in marriage."

Marriage?

Shock left her momentarily speechless. For a minute she thought she was weightless. Ready to take wing. She all but lost her breath. Hot blood rushed to her face. She felt wildly elated, astonished, wanting to follow wherever he went yet fearful of the consequences. She put trembling fingers to his lips. "Corin, *no*!" she whispered, as though their futures were already in jeopardy. "You must think of the fall-out!" His was no ordinary family. Dalton Rylance was an industrial giant. Corin was his son and heir. Her heart was beating so fast she might have been running…running…running.

But Corin wanted to marry her! She wanted to give herself up to the ecstasy, but terror stripped it back.

"Do you love me or don't you?" He gripped her shoulders, very much the dominant male.

She heard the hard challenge in his tone. She took a deep breath. "You know I love you. It's just that I can't keep seem to keep up with all the shocks! I'm thrilled out of my mind you want to marry me. I'm honoured. But you must see better than I how talk of marriage right now might affect Leila? When it comes to you, I don't think she's quite sane."

"Ah, to hell with Leila!" he cried, near violently. "She might go after what she wants, but so do *I*. I want *you*."

"You have no *doubts*?" It was almost impossible to centre herself, so high was she soaring.

"None whatsoever!"

"When we know Leila is the enemy? One who will stop at

nothing? She made her position very plain to me. If she is to suffer any consequences, she'll make sure we all do. She could hurt the people I love as a way of hurting me. There could be public scandal. A huge rift in the family. And what of your standing in Rylance Metals? Could that be undermined? We're dealing with a woman who would lie and lie and lie. The most outrageous lies are often believed. I believed all my life my grandparents were my parents."

A wave of anger for what had been done to *all* of them swept him. "Your grandparents were good people, doing everything they could to protect you. You had a happy, stable childhood. It shows. You might consider I'd suffer much more if I heeded your concerns about Leila. If secrets are to come out, let them. Hold them up to the light of day. There's nothing and no one who could make me give you up."

She felt like weeping at the depth of emotion in his face, in his voice. Love from Corin, when her mother was spitting hate. "Maybe it's best if I go home."

"Well, yes, I want you home," he confirmed strongly. "But of course Leila has the greatest chance of tracking our every movement there. Not that I care. We have to deal with her sooner or later. She might be crazy mad, but not mad enough to risk having her story come out. Dad isn't a man to privately let alone publicly humiliate. Leila could well get more than she bargained for."

"Would you like to unmask her?" She lifted her eyes to him, loving him with all her heart, but knowing Leila had caused a shift in the landscape.

"Yes," he said with certainty. "But I want *you* more than I could ever want to bring Leila unstuck. It's as Zara and I have told you. We abide by your decision. The fact that Leila is your mother is irremediable. We can't change it. We can work around it. She's not a fool. She's got very used to being rich. The houses, the clothes, the jewellery, the travel."

"So we lie to your father?" She broke gently away. She couldn't think clearly with his arms around her. "You want me to live a lie? I suppose I have to. I can imagine the effect on him if I told the truth. It could destroy their marriage!"

"Forgive me if I don't think it a tragedy," Corin said caustically, fuelled by frustration. He wanted Miranda desperately, yet knew she was withholding some part of herself. "You can't have it both ways, Miranda. You can't protect your mother *and* not suffer some harm to yourself."

"But think what a huge target I'd make if we suddenly announced our engagement." Her turquoise eyes dominated her small face. "*Think* of it. You're a Rylance. Dalton Rylance's heir. The press would want to know everything about me. They'd send some hotshot reporter to check on me and my background."

He had given that situation plenty of consideration. If Leila overnight suddenly revealed she had been triumphantly reunited with her long-lost daughter, all hell would break loose.

"Corin, you *must* listen." Her eyes had been truly opened to her mother. She was chillingly self-centred.

He lifted a quelling hand. "Let me work it out, Miranda. There has to be a resolution. You don't want your mother brought to account. So be it. The press side of it can be handled. We have people whose job is to take care of that. No one has unearthed any story on Leila, for a start. Very likely my father saw to that. Any story can be killed if enough influence is brought to bear. My father is a very powerful man. You really don't know how powerful. He's an industrial giant. God knows what fairy tale Leila told him, but if he didn't entirely swallow it he certainly took care of it. I'll take care of this."

He gave her a little space of time, then he went to her, drawing her into his arms. "I think I'd die without you." He bent to kiss her, the touch of his mouth exquisitely tender.

She felt its imprint right through her body. He kissed her under the chin, along her neck, making every pulse jump and her eyes glisten with tears.

"Do you believe, as I do, there's only *one* person for us in life, Miranda?" He laid a tender hand on her breast. "*One* person out there for us to find. Some never manage it, no matter how hard they search for their soul mate. The *blessed* do. That's how I feel about you. You're my *one* person. We can and will marry. And no one will be allowed to stand in our way."

CHAPTER EIGHT

THE Peninsula Beijing was his father's five-star hotel of choice when in the great city on business. It boasted everything he wanted. Understated elegance, top-notch amenities and an English-speaking staff. To keep Leila happy there was a luxury shopping arcade where she could spend his money to her heart's content. His father never set a limit on her.

Queensland's vast mineral resources and its mining boom had earned mining magnates like his father enormous wealth. Dalton Rylance's total preoccupation was making money. Huge profits for Rylance Metals. Corin had been arguing strongly for some time now for the industry to tackle other issues that needed to be acted on. Like promoting a higher standard of living for their mining communities for a start. God knew, enough money was being generated. He had been speaking on an off to other members of the board, taking the issue right to them, and been gratified to learn they weren't turning a deaf ear like his father. Such a high level of prosperity demanded the big players like Rylance address problems within the industry. When his day came—hopefully before then—that would certainly be the case.

China was a monolith. A great power and a most highly valued trading partner. Their negotiations with one of its leading corporations had spun out for several additional days. There were difficulties, always difficulties, trying to arrange a "marriage", but finally they had an outcome that both parties could agree on. A significant mining investment in Rylance Bauxite would be made. A decision that had brought a hugely satisfied smile to his father's handsome face.

"Great idea of yours, son, learning Mandarin like our PM," he said proudly, punching Corin's shoulder. "By the way, Lee wants to take us in his private plane to the Anhui Provence. We haven't been there. The landscape is supposed to be magnificent—lots of scenic wonders Leila might enjoy. Great men were born in the province, I understand, and it's famous for its arts and crafts—that sort of thing. I'd like you to come. Liang wants you along as well. He's formed a very high regard for you."

"And me for him," Corin said sincerely. "I'll think about it, Dad."

"Do," Rylance urged. "Regular flights shuttle around, of course, but Lee loves piloting his own plane. He knows the whole province like the back of his hand. I'd like us all to enjoy it—and his hospitality."

Leila carried her burning rage with her to the ancient city. It was a rage that she had never experienced before. She had watched Corin sidestep any number of the suitable young women that inhabited his privileged circle. She had used to congratulate herself on how she had helped see them off. Now everything had changed.

Miranda had entered their lives. Miranda—her own daughter. The turn of events defied belief. She suddenly saw Corin, the object of her long-held sexual desire, being taken away from her. Her infatuation for him had never diminished.

It had only grown stronger over the years. Corin had matured into the whole man: brilliant, stunning good looks, charm, impressing everyone who came his way. She hated the way she felt sometimes. Hated it. It was like being held in bondage. The very fact she was dealing with her own daughter demanded she show mercy, but she had to be a monster, because she couldn't manage a flicker. It was Miranda who had captured Corin's attention. Miranda who had come between her and her fatal obsession. Miranda needed punishing.

For some little time now she had felt Dalton's desire for her lessening. It had been *years*, after all. She counted on maintaining her beauty unimpaired until at least forty-two, forty-three. There were so many aids. But youth, unmatchable youth, never to be regained, was on her daughter's side. Miranda was exquisitely pretty. How ridiculous, then, was her ambition to become a doctor? That lofty profession was very much part of Jason's family.

There—she'd thought it. *Jason!* She had hardly given him a thought in twenty years, until that shocking night in London when she had turned around to see him reincarnated in his daughter. There were, after all, genes. It was to be expected. Miranda was so much like him, and his sister Roslyn. The resemblance was amazing. It had struck her dumb with fear.

Leila forced herself to take several deep breaths. Dalton was full of this trip to the Anhui Province. She was expected to go. They did everything together. And Dalton wanted Corin to accompany them. In many ways, Dalton idolised his son. He was enormously proud of him. When the time came Dalton was convinced Rylance Metals would be in safe hands.

Leila made a snap decision. She pivoted on her stiletto heels, going to the door of the suite. Dalton had gone for drinks with a couple of his American cronies, also in Beijing on business. With any luck at all Corin might still be in his room. Only one way to find out. Pay him a visit.

Corin answered the light tap on the door, only to find Leila, of all people, hovering with every appearance of nervousness. That was a first.

"Dad's not here, Leila," he told her briskly. "That's if you've come to find him and not corner me? He's having a drink with Hank Gardner and his business partner."

"I know." She expelled a quick breath. "May I come in?"

Corin's smile was faintly twisted. "What? Aid and abet a designing woman? I'm sorry, Leila, I'm just about to go out. What is it you want, anyway?"

"It's about Miranda," she said, actress that she was, managing to force tears into her eyes. "I may have deserted her, but I do care about her, you know."

"Yeah, right! Give me a break, Leila!" Corin continued to mock, his sexual presence so strong, so exciting, she wanted to throw herself at him, be gathered up in his arms. His youth—he was not yet thirty—his devastating good looks and the enormous energy that radiated off him only underscored the fact her husband was ageing.

"Please, please, just let me inside for a moment," she pleaded. "We have to talk. Really it's for the best." She managed to push past him, hurrying into the room, where she settled herself in an armchair, pressing down on its sides because her hands were shaking so much. This was her last-ditch stand. "Are you serious about my daughter?"

"Your *daughter*?" Corin scoffed. "That's right—so she is. You've been a great mother, Leila. All that money you sent to help out. Well, listen, and listen up well. I'm madly, deeply and irrevocably in love with Miranda. I intend to marry her."

Leila reacted as if he had shot a deadly arrow that had hit its mark. "You *can't*." A look of extreme pain crossed her face. *Real* pain. He hadn't known she was capable of it. "I won't allow it."

"How can you possibly stop it?" He gave her a long, challenging look.

"I'll go to Dalton," she said, throwing up her burnished head. "I'll confess my past."

"What? Version Two? He might well ask how many versions there are. I know you enjoy your power over him, Leila, but do you really believe you can sell him another sob story?"

Leila glanced about wildly. "I know how to handle your father, Corin. Miranda may look like butter wouldn't melt in her mouth, but she's a born schemer. She went after you like I went after your father. She freely admitted it to me. Proud of it, actually. We're two of a kind, you see."

"Quite sure of that, are you?" Corin remained standing, looking down at her with a vestige of Miranda's pity.

"She wants ten million to go away," Leila announced with great intensity. "That's sterling, would you believe? I told her I couldn't possibly put my hands on an amount like that. She then started to talk increments. She was relishing her power over me, her own mother. She said she would go to Dalton and give him the true story. How I abandoned her and my parents. Left them to rear her. No word from me. Ever. I told her in return for the money she would have to give you up completely. I have to be able to trust her, you see."

"Takes one sinner to know another," he mocked.

"True." Leila's face brightened. "She's quite the little con-woman."

"Is she, now?" Corin gave her a hard stare. "Leila, *I'm* worth a great deal more than ten million in any currency. Wouldn't she do better sticking with me?"

"But she doesn't *love* you, my dear!" Leila's voice rose, verging on hysteria. The room was swimming before her eyes. "She told me. She used you. She's been planning her revenge all these years. She wants to ruin me. Surely you realise that? You have to trust me, Corin. I care too much about you to see you get hurt. You would have no future with Miranda. It wouldn't take you long to see her in a different light. She would repulse you. No, don't shake your head. You should have been there when she was talking to me. It was a revelation. She *enjoyed* seeing me suffer."

And there it was, he thought. What he hadn't considered. Leila *was* suffering as she had made others suffer. He could *almost* find it in his heart to feel sorry for her. Only there was his mother. And Zara. And her attack on Miranda. "Leila, the last thing Miranda wants is to see you suffer," he said, his expression grave. "You're far too self-centred, too self-absorbed to see that. Miranda is a creature of the light. She's beautiful, tender, capable of giving great joy. I'm going to marry her. You need to accept that."

But Leila couldn't accept it. She had allowed her obsession to grow and flourish. "I never will!" She shot to her feet, her tortured expression showing the full depth of her futile passion.

"Leila, you know you have to drop this matter," Corin said urgently. "For your own sake. I've seen Dad turn on people. It's like watching a guillotine come down. You must get over this stupid infatuation, whatever it is. I am *not* and never have been attracted to you. What we have to do now is get a handle on the whole situation. Miranda refuses to see your life destroyed. You're her *mother*. *Your* mother continued to care deeply about you to her dying day. Miranda is respecting her grandmother's wishes as well. She must have been a fine woman, your mother. She brought Miranda up beautifully."

"But you've got entirely the wrong idea of Miranda!" Leila cried fiercely, not to be swayed. "Revenge has dominated her life. I'll tell you this, Corin, and mark my words—I'll break up my own marriage before I let you marry Miranda." Her golden-brown eyes glittered with real tears. "You won't come out well over this. We both know your father's temper. The way it bubbles up in him, then explodes. He won't let his plans for you go by the board. He has his mind set on that Atwood girl. He would never accept Miranda. You could be doing yourself and your career great damage."

Corin shook his head. "I don't think so. But that's a risk I'm prepared to take. Nothing in this world will stop me. I love Miranda. I honour and respect her. I loved her from the moment I laid eyes on her. Which you should know was nearly four years ago. Miranda could have gone to my father then. She didn't. She came to me. She wants to be a doctor. She will be a doctor. She has what it takes. As for me, I'll be very happy to have a doctor in the family. You should know I'm going to track down her father's family. It's up to Miranda, of course, if she wants to make contact."

Leila's face turned ashen. "You fool! Men are such fools!" She rose, then stalked past him, head up, her bronze eyes filled with anger and loathing. "You may not believe me yet, Corin, but my daughter is playing you for all she's worth. It happens. I should know. I played your father."

"And you contributed to the death of my mother." Corin's voice was a whiplash across her back. "Get out, Leila. Do your worst. I assure you, it won't be half good enough."

* * *

It was just after ten in the morning London time when the news came through.

> Australian mining magnate Dalton Rylance killed in a light airplane crash in China.

The newsflash posted on the Internet went on to report that Mr Rylance, his wife, Leila, and two other passengers, one believed to be Rylance's son Corin, had all been killed, along with the experienced pilot, the greatly respected Dr Lee Zhang, CEO of CMDC, a leading Chinese resource and development company.

Miranda was having coffee with Peter and his friend Natalia when Zara texted a message for her to go home immediately, where she would soon join her.

"What's that all about?" Peter asked, his high forehead creasing with worry. "Must be serious for Zara to send you a message like that."

Miranda, who had been enjoying Natalia's account of her accompanying a budding young diva, suddenly lost all colour. For long moments she was panic stricken, with streams of images flowing through her mind. None of them good. "It must be something to do with the China trip."

Peter thought so too. "We'll come with you," he said instantly. "At least see you home."

"I'll fix this." Natalia pushed back her chair, ready to make her way into the coffee shop to pay the bill. "There could be other reasons, Miri." She tried to offer comfort.

"I don't think so," Miranda answered. "I know this isn't good."

"Wait until you speak to Zara," Peter advised. "You don't really have any idea."

"I'm so afraid I do, Peter." Miranda's small white face was very still.

Zara had already arrived back at the house when Miranda arrived. She opened the door to them, her beautiful face, like Miranda's, pale and stricken.

"No—oh, no!" Miranda tried to ward off what was surely coming. She stood on the top step as though petrified. Peter and Natalia were frozen behind her. Clearly the news was very bad indeed.

"Come in. Come in," Zara urged. Her slender figure was swaying. "You too, Peter, and your friend." She tried to smile at Natalia.

"What is it? What's happened?" Peter asked, aghast, keeping one eye on Miranda. She looked as if she was about to faint.

Zara didn't answer. She didn't have the strength. She beckoned them into the drawing room, where she gave them the news.

"Father has been killed in a light aircraft crash in Anhui Province in China," she told them, chilling them through. "A distinguished Chinese businessman was the pilot. Leila was with Father, as usual, and there were two other passengers. The plane came down in the hills. No survivors."

"God!" Peter blurted out, flinching with shock.

"But this is dreadful news!" Tears of sympathy sprang into Natalia's green eyes. "Miri?" she cried out in alarm. "Miri?"

Galvanised, Peter got an arm around Miranda before she hit the floor. He held her for a moment, then settled her into an armchair. "Put your head down, Miri. There's a good girl.

Nat—" he appealed to his friend "—can you make us all tea? You can find the kitchen."

"Don't worry." Efficient in all things, Natalia moved off, controlling her own shock. Did this mean Zara's father, stepmother *and* her adored brother Corin had all been killed? It was too horrible to contemplate. Miranda looked as badly affected as Zara. Peter hadn't said much, but she had gained the impression Miranda and Corin Rylance had a strong connection. That had to be so.

An hour later Zara's mobile rang. They had stopped answering the incessant landline phone calls. It was always the press, avid for news and hopefully some comment from family on the other end.

"*Who?* Who is it?" There was a fearful catch in Miranda's voice. The shock was so violent even tears wouldn't come. Peter and Natalia, on call for rehearsal, had left some time earlier, still reeling with dismay, leaving the two distraught young women to try and comfort one another.

Under Miranda's stunned gaze, Zara's grief-stricken expression eased. She looked as though the worst had been averted. Faint colour returned to her cheeks. With her great dark eyes fixed on Miranda's face, she passed across her mobile.

And, with that, Miranda spoke to Corin.

Corin brought his father's and Leila's bodies home in a corporate jet, and they rested overnight in the Rylance family mansion.

The morning of the combined funerals dawned in glorious sunshine. A State funeral had been graciously declined by the family, although mourners dressed in black, with Dalton Rylance's colleagues all wearing black armbands, came from near and far to fill the cathedral to capacity, so it might as well have been. Everyone, right up to the State Premier, was filled with shock. The terrible suddenness of it all—the unexpectedness. Dalton Rylance had been only fifty-eight, a man in his prime, and his beautiful wife Leila some twenty years younger. They had been such a devoted couple. Dalton Rylance had strode the business scene like a colossus. No one had been prepared for it.

Such a tragedy! Now all eyes were on his son and heir, Corin, formidable in his iron-clad grief. His beautiful sister, Zara, back from London for the funeral and to be close to her beloved brother, stayed by his side. As did a young woman called Miranda Thornton, understood to be a Rylance Foundation recipient. Not a classic beauty, as was Zara Rylance, but immensely pretty. Neither Corin nor Zara Rylance did anything to hide their ease with her. Indeed, both appeared as though they were trying to protect her. She might well have been family.

It was something that alerted a lot of people. Indeed, many turned to stare after Miranda. She would be difficult to miss with her eye-catching head of silver-gilt curls.

Decisions, pressures and obligations came upon Corin from all directions. The responsibilities that accompanied being a Rylance. He scarcely had a minute to mourn.

Zara stayed on for a month, before she had to return to London to hand in her notice. There was no longer any need to live and work fourteen thousand miles away. She could come home. There was plenty for her to do. It was agreed she would wind up her affairs in London, then return.

Miranda elected to remain in Australia. Her mother's death had hit in her unexpected ways. The what *ifs?* Although at the same time she knew those "what ifs" would never have happened. Leila had taken what she had really wanted out of life. Not her daughter. Leila had craved the rich husband, the social prestige. She'd had it all for a while. Still, Miranda found herself grieving. Death was so final. No chance to work things out. She realised she *had* entertained a glimmer of hope.

Never mind, Miranda! that familiar voice said inside her head. *You were kind to her when other daughters mightn't have been. You chose to let Leila keep her secrets. She died with them.*

One increasing difficulty since the funeral was that the media had decided to take an interest in Miranda. Something she hadn't been looking for. It was worrying. Now she was linked to the Rylance family, they might start to concentrate their attention on her. What could they learn? She'd been born and raised on a small country farm. Her parents had been respectable community people. She had always been clever, an exceptional student. She had been awarded a scholarship by the Rylance Foundation to study for her Bachelor of Science degree, which she had attained with high distinction. In the year to come she was to take Medicine. Her ambition was clearly to become a doctor. Well, good doctors were desperately needed…

Harmless enough stuff surely? Only some reporters chasing a good story were unstoppable. That very morning, when she'd left Zara's riverside apartment where she was staying, it had been to find a member of the press camped outside.

"Staying in Miss Rylance's apartment, are you, love?" A cheeky-looking young man wearing a press badge swiftly closed in on her as she went to her small car, parked on the street.

"Is that any of your business?" She swung on him, so frazzled she wanted to hit him with her handbag.

He held up his hands. "Be reasonable now, love. Only asking a simple question."

Miranda faced him, a warning sparkle in her eyes. "First

of all, I am not your *love*. Zara Rylance is my friend. I'm looking after the apartment for her. Does that answer your question? You might step out my way. There are laws against harassment."

"Hang on. Hang on. Who's harassing you? I don't much care for that."

"And *I* don't much care for your hanging about outside," she responded sharply. "I'm nobody you could be interested in."

"Can't be a *nobody*, love, and a friend of the Rylances." He smirked. "Could Corin Rylance have an interest in you, by any chance?"

Miranda forced a peal of laughter. Never again would she be caught off guard. "You've got to be joking!"

The reporter pulled back. "You're saying he isn't?"

"I'm saying you're on the wrong track, pal." She managed another derisive laugh. "Bye, now!"

It might be wise for Corin to stay away from her altogether. He had more than enough to contend with. As always her first thought was for him.

Corin had left it late, using a different car from his own Mercedes and parking in Zara's double spot in the basement car park. No one was around. In the car park, or in the lift that took him to the penthouse level. There were two apartments. One belonged to a prominent businessman and his wife, well-known to the family and trusted, the other was Zara's. There were all sorts of problems he had to face, then somehow solve. Prioritising took precious time and there was more to come. A long-time member of the board had been so upset by the death of his father he had given notice of his retirement. That meant finding the right replacement. He had his eye on someone. Young, like himself, but with the intellect and the business acumen to take him far.

The weeks following the death of his father had been so labour intensive he'd scarcely had a minute to dwell on his grief. And grief it was. He had no idea, nor would he ever know, if Leila had carried out her threat to blacken Miranda's name and thus save her own. His father had appeared only mildly irritated by his decision not to join them on the Anhui Province trip, so he'd known nothing then. Corin prayed he never had. His father had failed him and Zara in many ways—certainly he had broken their adored mother's heart—but he had loved him and greatly admired his razor-sharp brain.

This current invasion of privacy was hard to take, but it was one of the hazards of public life. Miranda had already told him she didn't want the media anywhere near her. He knew she feared her whole sorry story would come out, but he had his PR people controlling the flow of information. The last thing either of them wanted at this point was press speculation on a possible love affair. Worse, a love-nest. He couldn't bear the thought of Miranda being hounded. Anyone in the extended family who had raised doubts about his stepmother in the distant past had been told very firmly to keep their mouths shut. His grandparents *had* to know, but to his eternal relief after the first resounding shock they'd rallied. If there was a price to pay for Leila's deceptions they were united in their belief her abandoned daughter shouldn't have to pay it. Genealogy had to be put to one side.

His grandparents had met Miranda at the reception held at the house after the funeral. They'd had no idea of her true identity then. At the time they had confided they found themselves "quite taken" with Zara's little friend—indeed felt curiously protective of her. They didn't know exactly why. Miranda really was a child of light, Corin thought. His grandparents had had no difficulty seeing it. If anything, they were full of good will. Miranda might be Leila's daughter, but over and above that she was *herself*.

Corin moved Miranda into the living room before he took her in his arms. Every time he hugged her it was to realise she had lost weight. It wouldn't do for a featherweight like Miranda.

"I've a suggestion." He had lost much of his tension in one single kiss. "A friend of mine has a great hideaway on the Gold Coast. I can't send you to our place, obviously. You wouldn't have any peace or privacy. Dave and his wife are in Los Angeles at the moment. They'll be away for six months or so. They're more than happy to let you stay in their beach house. Secluded, a short walk to the beach."

Miranda turned up her face, her sombre mood lightened just with his presence. "Sounds good to me."

"You need the break."

"I do. Life is so fragile, isn't it? Sometimes it seems as though it's hanging by a mere thread. What would I have done, Corin, if you had gone on that fatal trip? The very thought is a terror."

He clasped her tighter. He had picked up on her depressed mood the instant he had walked through the door. She really did need to get away. "It's been an ordeal. That's why the beach house seems like the answer. Somewhere quiet and beautiful, tranquil, where you can shut down all the images that are passing through your head. I share those images. Both of us have lost a parent. It's a milestone in life. And this was a particularly bad way for them all to go. Dr Zhang was an experienced pilot, in apparent good health. No one could have foretold he would have a stroke at the controls."

"There's no total security anywhere," she said. "You can be in the wrong place at the wrong time. He would have survived had he been back in Beijing. They all would."

"No one can control fate, Miranda," he said gently. "Profound fears for the safety of our loved ones are part of life. Those fears, at least, we can and must control. You need peace and quiet. No one to bother you like they're starting to bother you here. You'll have the sun and sea, dazzling white sand. We have it all at our doorstep there. We've known its healing power since we were kids. It's a glorious spot. You can surf, go for long walks, read, drive up to Marina Mirage to shop. I'll call you every day. I'll come to you at the weekend. You look exhausted." Very gently he touched the mauve shadows beneath her beautiful eyes.

"Not sleeping," she confessed, pressing her mouth against his hand. "Not eating much either. Not hungry. First time ever. I've always had a good appetite. The accident killed it. And those horrendous moments when Zara and I thought you were on the plane too. Maybe we shouldn't love too much," she said in an unsteady voice. "To love is to risk losing. The more intense the love, the greater the risk. I never knew my mother, Corin, yet I'm mourning her. I'm mourning your father. The only way I can describe it is to say I feel…*hulled*."

He pressed her silver-gilt head against his chest. "Oh, Miranda! If only I could go with you, but that isn't possible," he groaned.

"I know. I'm not asking."

He held up her chin. "You take too much on yourself. You can't carry your natural capacity for caring beyond certain boundaries. You'll have to do it when you're a doctor."

"I know! But such a lot has happened. Losing my grandparents—especially my grandmother—was a terrible experience. Then Leila and your father. What if I'd lost *you*?" Her voice broke in anguish.

"Well, you didn't. I'm here." He gathered her against his heart. She clung to him. His Miranda. He lowered his head to kiss her, this young woman he cherished. "Love you. Love you. Love you."

The fervent admission was deeply thrilling. Within moments all the sadness that had beset Miranda vanished like morning mist. Heat ran through her veins. Soon an overwhelming desire lapped them in a ring of fire. She was transported to another world, a world with only the two of them in it.

"I'm not going anywhere either," Corin muttered against her parted lips. "You're stuck with me."

She lay on the sofa, where he had carried her. He sat at her head, quite comfortable on the floor. Her hand was delicately tracing the outline of his face. "I love you so much it frightens me, Corin. I feel ashamed, too, for showing my weakness. I know the demands on your time. No demands are being made on me."

He made a little scoffing sound. "Carrying around multiple griefs is a demand. You've had a series of powerful shocks, Miranda. Dad's end was so sudden and violent we're all affected. Even the staff are traumatised. Everyone is walking around in a near trance. Dad always appeared indestructible. Now he's gone. Just like that! God knows, I'm finding it difficult to keep my mind ticking over."

"Of course. I'm sorry, Corin." She turned her head, bolstered by a few silk cushions, towards him. "Do you think she told him? That question haunts me."

"We've been over that, Miranda. The answer is *no*!" He

spoke firmly, catching her fingers and holding them tight. No point whatever in dwelling on the possibility that Leila might have, he thought.

"It's hard coming to terms with death, isn't it?" she said very quietly.

Love for her pierced his heart. She had known too much sadness. He was going to change that. "We have one another now, Miranda. That means *everything*!"

"Everything to me too," she whispered, her voice very soft.

"I want Zara back home as soon as possible. She's given in her notice. Her colleagues are sorry to see her go, but they understand."

"She's coping," Miranda said, glad that was so. She and Zara were in frequent contact. "One loves one's parents even if they don't always treat us kindly. Why don't I get you a drink?" she asked with haste. She would have got him one long before this, but their lovemaking had taken precedence over all else. "I've got plenty of food in the fridge. Salmon fillets, scallops, fresh crab meat. Everything we need for a salad. I thought we could sit out on the balcony." Miranda sat upright, straightening her short, loose dress, a lovely water-colour print that tied on the shoulders like a little girl's dress. It was a style back in fashion.

She swung her legs to the floor. A beautiful breeze was blowing in from the balcony. She walked to the open sliding doors, looking out across the plant-filled area at the night-time glitter. City towers on the skyline, apartment blocks, wonderful old buildings, bridges that spanned the broad, deep river, the City Kats moving passengers smoothly from the inner suburbs to the city, rippling dark waters shot with multi-coloured reflected light—blue, orange, red, gold and silver. The breeze coming off the water was as soft as a silk banner against her bare skin.

"I'm staying the night." Corin joined her, sliding his arms around her, his breath warm against her cheek.

"Marvellous!" She didn't think she would ever get enough of him. Her guardian angel must have been watching over her the day she met Corin.

His warm mouth burnished the tender skin of her nape.

"You don't think we should be cautious?" she asked very quietly, always concerned for him.

"Right now I'm beyond caution," he murmured. "I'm *passionate* for you. I can't let you go."

She spun in his arms. "You're not worried someone will spot you when you leave? You do rather stand out," she smiled. He was a *prince*!

"A small risk. I don't want to walk alone any more, Miranda," he said very seriously. "I need you with me. Every step of the way."

She wanted to cry. "Then that's a miracle, Corin." Her heart was in her eyes.

"A miracle that humbles me. Can I just say this—and I don't want you to be cross—?"

"Say whatever you want. Don't keep anything to yourself. No secrets. Not any more."

She swallowed on a little dry patch in her throat. He *had* to know. She had no choice. "I know you've tried to reassure me, but I can't help agonising over whether you're shoving my true identity to the back of your mind? You must give me a truthful answer, Corin. Do you think it possible it could surface over time?"

"Miranda!" He released her name on a long, agonised exhalation.

"Let me finish. Time brings changes. We both know that. You're taking me into *your* world. It's a vastly different world from the one I grew up in. We must be clear on this. I know you love me. Lord knows I love you. The magic of it has kept me safe. And sane, I should tell you. There has been a lot to handle. It's just that I can't help feeling—actually *knowing*—your life would be so much easier, less problematic, without me."

"Stop it, Miranda!"

"But it's eating at me. What if someone tracks me down? Don't they always say the truth will out?" She held his glittering, dark eyes. "You could be letting yourself in for a lot, Corin. It's a bizarre story—like something out of a movie—and we can't escape it."

He lifted a hand to silence her. "We can and we *will*!" he said with great authority. "No more of this, Miranda. With you at my side, nothing is beyond me. I would want you whatever the cost. Surely you know that? At its worst what would it be? A nine-day wonder? If Leila left any tracks, Dad covered them. I can do the same. Besides, it's *me* you're worrying about, not yourself. I won't have it. You're everything in the world to me. There's no going back. There's only *forward*!"

He sounded so strong, so utterly sure of himself and *her*, and her own waning courage was restored. She wasn't physically like her mother. Her nature was very different. What more was there to know?

"Come to bed," Corin urged in a deep, desirous voice. "Just holding you in my arms is the most perfect feeling in the world." Gently he pulled at the ties on her shoulders. Her loose dress, a series of ruffles, landed gently in an iridescent pool at their feet.

"You're beautiful, so beautiful!" He cupped her breasts, letting the pads of his thumbs encircle the nipples.

The merest touch and she was aflame, her body flooding with sensation.

His voice had dropped to a deep, yearning pitch. "You're

like some exquisite figurine wrought out of alabaster. You're more than I deserve, Miranda."

"No, that isn't so!" Such a tumult of emotion rose inside her it was like a starburst. Against the catastrophe in their lives, they could set the miracle of their love.

It was the wheel of fortune in motion. If she hadn't found her mother she would never have found Corin. So in the end it was Leila who had brought Corin into her life. There was grace in that.

Her arms trembling, Miranda reached up to lock them around his neck. "I give myself into your hands completely," she said with such fervour it became a vow. "You are my love. My lover. My life!" It was the ultimate expression of trust. And with the giving came a hitherto unattainable *peace* and acceptance. Corin had made his choice in life. He wanted *her* for his wife. That was the greatest honour of all.

The radiance of her expression made Corin's breath catch in his throat. He swept her up into his arms, in that moment no mere man but a god, exultant. He stood for a moment, locking in the memory of her at that precise moment. Then he carried her down the hallway to the quiet of the master bedroom, where he would peel from her what single garment remained, spread her alabaster body on the bed, silver-gilt head against the pillows, before he sank onto her.

Kissing would pass to prolonged caresses...little whispered endearments to moans...soon the rapture would become too intense for them. It wasn't simply a matter of two people becoming physically one. It was an exchange of *souls*. Corin knew deep within himself he could surmount any and every problem that might confront them. It was the *future* that beckoned, luminous with light, rich with promise.

Life was a tapestry composed of many strands: love, loss, sorrow, happiness, success, failure. There was only one way to handle it—take up the tapestry with both hands. Miranda had given great depth to his existence. He considered himself truly blessed. No greater gift could a woman give to her man than her *heart*.

No one in this world would look after Miranda's tender heart better than he.

Coming Next Month

Available October 12, 2010

#4195 CATTLE BARON NEEDS A BRIDE
Margaret Way
The Rylance Dynasty

#4196 AMERICA'S STAR-CROSSED SWEETHEARTS
Jackie Braun
The Brides of Bella Rosa

#4197 COWGIRL MAKES THREE
Myrna Mackenzie
Rugged Ranchers

#4198 A MIRACLE FOR HIS SECRET SON
Barbara Hannay

#4199 JUGGLING BRIEFCASE & BABY
Jessica Hart
Baby on Board

#4200 IF THE RED SLIPPER FITS...
Shirley Jump
In Her Shoes...

HRCNM0910

HARLEQUIN®
A Romance
FOR EVERY MOOD™

See below for a sneak peek at
our inspirational line, Love Inspired®.
Introducing HIS HOLIDAY BRIDE
by bestselling author Jillian Hart

Autumn Granger gave her horse rein to slide toward the town's new sheriff.

"Hey, there." The man in a brand-new Stetson, black T-shirt, jeans and riding boots held up a hand in greeting. He stepped away from his four-wheel drive with "Sheriff" in black on the doors and waded through the grasses. "I'm new around here."

"I'm Autumn Granger."

"Nice to meet you, Miss Granger. I'm Ford Sherman, from Chicago." He knuckled back his hat, revealing the most handsome face she'd ever seen. Big blue eyes contrasted with his sun-tanned complexion.

"I'm guessing you haven't seen much open land. Out here, you've got to keep an eye on cows or they're going to tear your vehicle apart."

"What?" He whipped around. Sure enough, mammoth black-and-white creatures had started to gnaw on his four-wheel drive. They clustered like a mob, mouths and tongues and teeth bent on destruction. One cow tried to pry the wiper off the windshield, another chewed on the side mirror. Several leaned through the open window, licking the seats.

"Move along, little dogie." He didn't know the first thing about cattle.

The entire herd swiveled their heads to study him curiously. Not a single hoof shifted. The animals soon returned to chewing, licking, digging through his possessions.

Autumn laughed, a warm and wonderful sound. "Thanks,

SHLIEXP1010

I needed that." She then pulled a bag from behind her saddle and waved it at the cows. "Look what I have, guys. Cookies."

Cows swung in her direction, and dozens of liquid brown eyes brightened with cookie hopes. As she circled the car, the cattle bounded after her. The earth shook with the force of their powerful hooves.

"Next time, you're on your own, city boy." She tipped her hat. The cowgirl stayed on his mind, the sweetest thing he had ever seen.

Will Ford be able to stick it out in the country to find out more about Autumn?
Find out in HIS HOLIDAY BRIDE
by bestselling author Jillian Hart,
available in October 2010
only from Love Inspired®.

SHLIEXP1010